WITCHITA STORIES

Troy James Weaver

Paperback ISBN 978-1-892061-73-7

Limited Hardcover Edition ISBN 978-1-892061-74-4

Cover and book design by Bryan Coffelt

Interior photographs by Chad Droegemeier

Printed in the United States of America

"There are moments, reading *Witchita Stories*, where everything dropped away, and I was speechless, or at least whatever the equivalent of speechless is when you're not talking in the first place. There is a deep sadness to these stories, and humor, but most importantly, honesty. This feels real and heavy and it's just about the best thing I've read in a long time."

—J. David Osborne, author of *Low Down Death Right Easy*

"*Witchita Stories* miraculously threads together small-town American aches into a fabric wholly warm, dirty, and alive. Weaver's literary mixtape is gentle yet trenchant, pained yet loving, scary yet funny as hell. Readers should hope that this book—our ghost story—lasts."

—Ken Baumann, author of *EarthBound*

"*Witchita Stories* melds together memory with the stories we keep to ourselves, the revelatory shade, the rude awakening. Weaver's voice is fresh yet familiar, a voice calling out from the bar late at night with a story that could almost be is ours. [I]t's the pitch-perfect mastery of Weaver's language that keeps us there, listening intently. "

—Michael J Seidlinger, author of *The Face of Any Other*

for my brother

SUMMER

My sister is sixteen and she's already at that stage in life where she's bringing over guys that look like Fonzie or Vanilla Ice. Some have tattoos, some have scars, some smoke cigarettes and listen to music that sounds like it's been ground up and shit out through a ripped subwoofer. You take a little walk one day, maybe down to the neighborhood park, and when you come back home, you find these dudes there with their t-shirts rolled up to show off their stupid tats, smoking cigarettes and kissing your sister on the front porch. Some have greasy hair, pulled back in a ponytail. Others have buzzed heads and goatees, and wear leather jackets and work boots. It is summer now, both parents at work, and my sixteen-year-old sister is too busy with her greaser on the porch to give a shit about what my brother and I are up to. She's the oldest, I'm the youngest, and my brother is lost somewhere between. One time she fed us macaroni and cheese, another time she fed us nothing. Today it is peanut butter licked from a spoon. Sometimes we spoon the peanut butter and dip it in the sugar bowl, but not today because somebody forgot to put sugar on the fucking grocery list. It's the hottest kind of summer in the Midwest.105. The humidity here will make you want to crawl into a freezer and lock the door. Don't worry about killing yourself; it'll be worth it. Just remember: that pedophile on your front porch won't always be there. But your sister will. Yes, she'll always be there, and until further notice she loves you the best she knows how, which must be enough, and you'll try loving her just the same. As for that peanut butter stuck to the roof of your mouth? Keep it there. It will be something to come back to when you're hunting for nourishment later on in life.

PCP

When he was in high school, my brother had this friend, a big redheaded dude with gnarly freckles. The first time I met the guy was late one night in our basement. He cracked the storm window sneaking in. There was another guy there too, but he looked more like an anorexic skeleton than anything, and besides, I knew him. This other guy, though—man, he was scary, with this wild hair and pale skin and loose clothes all black. His t-shirt said something about Cradle of Filth, and had this guy, just as pale as he was, staring out at me through scary dead eyes, no pupils, all white. I think I was twelve, I can't remember, but I'm sure I was no more than thirteen. I'd never even given a thought to what these types did in their spare time. Now there was no question about it. This big guy, he showed us a hole in his shin that looked infected, claiming it was the result of driving a nail in with a claw hammer. That's the way they all were. They wore their self-inflicted burns and cuts like they were notches in a bedpost. I never understood it, the cutting and burning, not yet. I had my demons too, though, and they weren't any less destructive. I threw my television out my bedroom window one day just because I couldn't find a decent show to watch. I stole road signs and decorated my room with them. I despised anybody who asked any questions, about anything, and I kept all of my brother's secrets. So this big dude with crazy red hair, I believed him when he told us about the nail in the leg, doing it just so he could go on feeling something. Later on, he moved on to not wanting to feel anything and pulled some pills from his sock, a whole fucking bottle, and crushed them up on a gaudy Christmas cookie tin. They took turns snorting between drags from shared cigarettes. Then things went fuzzy, chaotic, and I stood there, the loner, watching the sweat drip from their earlobes, wondering whose heart would be the first to collapse beneath the weight of the god-awful boredom of this place.

SMUT

My brother has this friend who only comes over when my parents aren't home. One day I walk in and they're watching porn together in the living room. Nothing gay, they're just watching. I try running up to my room before they notice me, but this friend of my brother's drags me down the stairs and pins me to the floor. My brother has disappeared, he's not there all the sudden, maybe he had to piss, and this friend of his is holding me down, saying: *Watch it! What are you, a faggot? Fucking watch it, you queer! Look!* Holding me down and prying at my eyes with his fingertips. *You fucking pussy, look at the big fucking cock on that dude! You like that, don't you? Look at her twat, you faggot!* And it seems to last forever. Whole lifetimes pass before me. My shoulders hurt, my eyes burn, and I feel like I could truly and honestly kill somebody at this point, anybody and for no reason at all. Finally, the kid flies right off of me, as though wind-lifted, and he looks all about the room, stunned. And I'm confused. What happened? But now *he's* on the ground, and my brother's on top of him, this kid's shoulders pinned now beneath his knees. *What the fuck! That's my little brother, you fuck!* My brother hits the dude. *Fuck you, you fucking—* He hits him again. *Fuck!* He spits in his face. Then, literally, and it's just like the movies, my brother picks this dude up by the shirt collar, drags him across the carpet, and throws him off the porch. He slams the door and looks me in the eyes, face red, gone blotchy. *Go to your room,* he says. I look at him, tears in my eyes, lips aquiver. *Go to your room!* I look at him again, hoping he sees I'm begging not to go. *Go,* he says, mouth movements slow and dramatic, and he steadies his eyes on the tits bouncing on the screen. *Go on*, he says. *Get the hell out of here.*

SMUT JR.

Later that year, after I'd turned fourteen, this same friend of my brother's, the one who'd pried my eyes to watch the videoed fucking, lived in our garage for almost two whole weeks. I guess they'd patched things up. He was only sixteen, a dropout, homeless now that his parents didn't want him anymore, and I guess my parents felt sorry enough for him to let him stay out in the garage on one of our old couches. I honestly don't remember seeing him all that often. He'd pop his head in, maybe eat a sandwich if we had the ingredients, and when his two weeks were up and gone, I thought: *Thank god I never have to see you again.* But maybe five years later, I recognized his name in the newspaper accompanied by a nice little mug shot. Formal charges had been brought against him for the murder of a young girl with a shotgun—not in Wichita, but down south somewhere. And now, I wonder if he knew, years earlier, sleeping in our garage, that he'd be a convicted killer someday. You know, when he grew up and started considering career options for his life.

FISHING

I used to go fishing when I felt like the world was sucking me down. I'd grab my tackle box and pole, grab a hat and fill an empty pop bottle with water, take off to where the street ended and became open fields, and go off knowing I'd just have me and my lonesome to deal with for the day, feeling content to live inside the empty rooms of my head. Sometimes a neighbor kid a couple years older than me would follow me out there. Sometimes I'd ditch him, sometimes he'd find me. This kid was annoying, that's for sure. My brother didn't like him much either. In fact he shot him with his BB gun when he was fourteen. And a few years later, when we were all a bit more mature, I received a tennis racket across my face for that little metal ball. I ditched him this time, the bastard, and took a different route altogether. When I got there, the smell of the lake was like breathing through an old unwashed sock, algae all over the place. I sprawled out on the bank, staring into the sun, fishing pole and tackle beside me, wondering, as my brother had told me, if this was really what a woman's womanly parts smelled like. I remember this vividly, this contemplation. And years later, when I got old enough to stick my nose down there and fumble around for myself, it took me back, that first waft, to the peaceful loneliness I'd experienced as a boy with a fishing pole, laying out across the weeds in the hot summer sun.

TEN FILMS

1. *Blue Velvet*

2. *A River Runs Through It*

3. *Un Chien Andalou*

4. *Days of Heaven*

5. *Sometimes a Great Notion*

6. *Wise Blood*

7. *River's Edge*

8. *The Lost Boys*

9. *Dumbo*

10. *Jurassic Park*

FIRST KISS

The first time I kissed a girl I was in fifth grade. I was staying the night at a friend's house. We set his tent up in the backyard. This would be where we would spend our night and eventually fall asleep. Earlier, we had hung out with two eighth-grade girls down the street. They smoked cigarettes and swore a lot. My first two kisses were with them. They snuck out of their houses in the middle of the night and came to our tent. The taller one with streaks in her hair pulled a plastic pop bottle from her purse. We began. They set the bottle down and I spun it, watching nervously, hoping it didn't land on my friend. I didn't want to kiss a dude. And I got lucky. It landed on the shorter girl with brown hair. I started with a quick peck. She took over and showed me how it was done. She shoved her tongue in my mouth. It tasted bad, probably from the cigarettes, but I didn't mind. I stuck my tongue in her mouth. This was happening. I looked over and saw my friend and the tall girl were kissing, too. I felt happy and nervous and dangerous. I kept thinking about how my parents would be really disappointed if they ever found out. But then I just stopped thinking altogether. Fuck it. We switched. I was kissing the tall girl now. She had bigger boobs. She put my hand on her boobs and brushed her hand across my penis a couple of times. After a while I was back with the short girl, the one I really liked. She was sweet, and I felt at home there in her arms, licking the smoke off her tongue. For a while, I convinced myself that this was what love felt like. I never saw either one of them again, can't even recall their names, but they meant enough to me that I'm putting them right here, on this page, so they can remain here, with me, forever, even in this small way.

RIOTS

The summer I turned twenty, my brother was out of prison for a few months and we got drunk with my dad one night—Jack and Cokes. I can't remember what happened or what was said, all I know is I ended up madder than hell and went after my brother with a steak knife.

Several minutes of struggle ensued.

When they finally got the knife free from my fist, I bolted up the staircase, trying my damnedest to get away from my brother's incredible prison bulk. But I wasn't quick enough. I could smell him behind me. His palm dwarfed my shoulder, and before I knew it I was thrown down the stairs. Every hard angle of the steps entered my body like a dull knife.

So there I am, sprawled out in a daze, thinking: *I deserved that,* and my brother is over by the table, trembling, saying *you deserved that, you fuck*, and my dad is back in his seat, sipping on his liquid and looking at us like we're crazy.

Fact is, my brother wasn't some little Goth kid anymore, but a prisoner, with shitty tats to boot, and every year he was looking more and more like the ones you catch late at night on Discovery Channel, when you can't seem get into the groove of your couch right.

When I miss him I fall asleep to the riots on the TV.

I remember putting a fishhook through his thumb when we were little kids, before all that ink and bars came between us, and feeling so bad I kissed it: the hole, the blood—and I'd do it again. In a heartbeat, just give me that goddamn thumb and I'll know and you'll know how much it is I really love him.

What's that boo-boo lip out for? Suck it up, I'd tell him. *Be a man.*

CLOTHING

It's hard to say exactly when my brother started wearing my sister's clothes. There was a moment there when everyone clearly ignored the fact that my sister's shirts and pantyhose were popping up around the house with ripped linings, loose threads, pit stains, runs. For a while nobody had the courage to confront this. Everybody kept their questions in that tight space inside their skulls. But gradually, as the weeks went by, it became clear to all of us that somebody much larger than my sister was certainly wearing her clothes. There could be no other explanation. Nobody could come up with a better one. It couldn't be Dad, he hated queers, and I was too small, unable to produce such damage, but my brother, my brother—he was the only explanation we could force from our denial-ridden lips.

If I'm not mistaken, he was wearing one of my sister's tight shiny shirts when he got caught sneaking back into the house one night. It was tight on her, so on him it was like a second skin. He had sweat all over him, stinging his eyes, coming out through his pants and running into her shirt, streaks upon streaks of sweat. It was summer. He had on scuffed Doc Martens and had both ears pierced, loop earrings, a dangling cross. He was always pushing those types of boundaries with fashion. To me it was some type of gay punk look with a slightly gothic spin. The sadness was there, the deep depression that manifests itself most poignantly through the lyrics of The Cure. As a younger brother, sometimes you take a look at your siblings and almost admire them for their boldness of vision, however borrowed it may be.

SEX ED

My brother was into witchcraft for a time, the occult of Crowley, the unholy trickery of the tarot. He started wearing black and plaguing himself with pentagrams, lipstick smears and eyeliner. He read books by Anton LaVey and produced poetry so dark it made Baudelaire seem like a pussy. His clothes became baggier and raggedy, only washed if my mother insisted. Some of them looked like mere rags. He wanted to look like a lowlife, and this fact didn't go unnoticed by anybody in the family, let alone the neighbors.

Our treehouse still stood in that outcropping of trees just minutes from our house. Little did I know that it was still a sanctuary for my brother— an incubator for his dabbling in perversities. But I had always been a pretty lonely kid, always seeking affection, and so when my brother invited me to his tiny castle in the woods, I went, not really caring one way or the other what we found ourselves engaged in there.

When we got out into the field near the creek, my brother produced a plastic bag, a big old Ziploc, the biggest I'd ever seen, and said: *We're frog hunting.* This actually wasn't an odd thing for me to take part in. I was an outdoorsy type I was when I was young, so I went at it fast and furious, scooping up frogs by the fistfuls down on the muddy banks and throwing them into the bag, not questioning the fate that lie ahead of them.

We must have had twenty in there by the time we made it up to the treehouse. It was about thirty or forty feet up, with foot-long scraps of two-by-four nailed into the trunk as a ladder. When we got inside my brother produced some kind of evil book of rituals and rites, slapped it on his lap and searched for the right page. I was observing the bag of frogs, holding it up, twisting it in the light, when he promptly ripped it from my hands. He had a kitchen pot up there, all scorched on the inside, and he started filling it with lighter fluid that he'd pulled from some secret compartment in his fortress. *What are you going to do?* I asked him. *Just watch,* he said, *and hold this book open, so I can read it.* He pulled out a match book, laid it beside him. *My god,* I thought. *We have to be quick about this, okay,* he said. *Now, just hold the book up so I can read it.* I didn't want to, but I held it up anyway. He lit a match and threw it into the pool of lighter fluid. The fire was a lot bigger than I had anticipated. Then he had the Ziploc bag open, dumping the frogs in before I could do something to stop him. I closed my eyes. The sound was indescribable—popping, hissing, tiny little screams—and the stench, the stench was unbearable. I opened my eyes in time to see a couple of them hop out of the flames, but they hadn't put themselves out, no, they were slow dying balls of fire. My brother hurriedly read from the book, words that would never mean anything to me, and then he clapped the lid over the flame and stomped out the few frogs that had escaped beneath his shoe. I wanted to cry, I wanted resurrection, but I also wanted my brother to love me, so instead I asked him, *What kind of spell did you cast?* And he tells me: *There's this girl at school I want to fuck.*

FEATHERS

There are people crowded into a room, all ages, teenaged kids to twenty- and thirty-somethings, some with their parents, some on their own, fifteen to twenty all counted. I'm there, too, hiding under a chair beside my parents, my brother and sister down the row. The guy leading the meeting looks like the real McCoy, a true Indian, or if you prefer: Native American. I didn't know what to call them, but this dude has got this long gray hair all done up in braided pigtails, a feather in it, and he's burning sage in a turtle shell and passing it around so that everybody present might receive a spiritual cleansing. When everybody has been washed in the smoke, he pulls the feather from his hair and explains the rules: *This is called a talking feather. Whoever is holding the feather is the only one allowed to say anything. Even if you want to interject you must wait until the feather has gotten around to you. I want everybody to be honest, not only about why they are here, but also about what they are going to do to make it out of here a better person. Okay.*

I think: *God, not another truth sermon,* and I listen to their stories with vague interest. To me it's just a bunch of people I never want to care about. Drunks, druggies, lesbians, gays, gangbangers, headbangers, Goths—they're all present. Then there are the parents, most of them just your average middle- to upper-middle class parents who've done their best for their children. Jesus, and there are mine, too, feeling defeated and mystified, but looking just as high and holy and caring as they ever have in any other situation. My dad has the same look on his face that he has when he watches baseball. How did things ever get this bad? Are they bad? Is this the new normal? It doesn't matter, not now. I'm in too deep. I listen to their stories—stories of desperation, betrayal, complete and utter despair, suicidal thoughts; Sandy selling favors for a snort; Johnny fucking the babysitter after she got him drunk one night when he was eleven or twelve years old; Tim not knowing his damage until he visited the doctor a few weeks ago and found out he's positive for hepatitis C; Sam talking about the enlarged liver of his deceased father and saying that he'll end up just like him: dead at forty and too poor to be interred in the family plot. You tend to get it all at these places, fuck-ups and wash-outs with brains like Swiss cheese, and you hate them all, especially since you are a little kid who has never experienced these things and don't quite know yet that the world is a place where you are supposed to feel afraid. But at the same time, you want to take their shoulders in your small young hands and shake them, you want to shake them until they fall from their old worn-out bodies and slip into some new ones. You want to grab that fucking feather and remind them that there is a child present. But you don't, and you feel stupid for it, because it's all clear now, all of it. Everything has come into view—fucking hypocrite. And now that you're older, you know you've become one of them—the people you loathed and kicked to shit in your head and wanted to throw into the garbage bin. And you feel guilty, ashamed. Your friends now go to meetings like these. And perhaps you should too. Who knows? You get fucked up each and every night, right? You don't look back. You don't look forward. You don't look at all. And your parents, they must have known you were checking under your bed for people at night, even while they were telling you there were no such things as monsters.

CONVERSATION OVERHEARD IN THE LINE AT THE GROCERY STORE

Woman (to Man): So…it was aborted?

Man: Think so.

Woman: How'd they afford that?

Man: Don't know. He hasn't had a job in two years.

Woman: And aside from that, abortion's just wrong.

Man: Shit—I forgot something!

Woman: What is it?

Man: Stay in line. I'll be right back.

Woman stands there behind the shopping cart, tapping a toe and humming a Katy Perry song.

A couple minutes later the man comes back with a carton of eggs.

Woman: What? You gonna make me an omelet?

Man: If you stay over tonight, you'll get more than just an omelet. (Nervous laughter.)

Woman: Hmm, we'll see.

The man touches the woman's ass as she hands the cashier her credit card.

FAVORITE FLOWERS

Scabiosa

Tulip

Rose

Dahlia

Chocolate Cosmos

Liatris

Ranunculus

Oriental Lily

Freesia

Peony

Godetia

SEXUAL
EXPERIENCE

The first one I saw that excited me was in a magazine. I suppose that's how a lot of boys see their first one. That goes for boobs too. And the second one was probably the same. But the third one was different. Or was it the fourth—fifth? Doesn't matter, this one wasn't in any magazine or video. It was my brother's girlfriend's sister's pussy and she was showing it to me out in the garage while my parents were gone for the weekend, visiting my great aunt in Nebraska. And honestly, it wasn't awesome. It looked like I knew it would look, which was cool, but I was embarrassed because she already had a bunch of hair going on down there. She was a woman. She was my own age and I only had this gross peach fuzz, my cock not yet grown into the fully functioning size of manhood. How does this happen? The first few naked women I'd seen made my penis hard, with the exception of the time I was forced to watch, but now I have this beautiful naked girl in front of me, showing me all of her goods, wanting me to touch her and make her come alive, and my penis does absolutely nothing—in fact, it feels retracted, sunken into my body, more dead than alive. She kind of laughed at me. She must have noticed my discomfort. *Don't be a wuss,* she said. *Come over here!* I had lumps all up in my throat. I resented her. *Get your pants on,* I said. *You aren't like that. Come on, stop acting like a slut and get your pants on.* But she didn't, she just lit up a cigarette, pants still crumpled around her ankles, and fondled her abnormally large tits through her t-shirt, so I started for the door. *Fine,* she said, *I'll just have to find someone else to fuck.* She looked more pissed than crushed, which annoyed me. *Whatever,* I muttered. I went to my bedroom and tried masturbating to the thought of her lying there beside me on my bed—not having sex, just lying there, caressing my hair and massaging my tiny muscles, but I couldn't do it, couldn't even get it hard. Truth is: she was too honest for my world. As for me, I was lying through my fucking teeth.

SURVIVAL

My brother has many afflictions and addictions, too many to count, really. There are just these corruptible things, just like other things, and they're all around us. I don't know where they stem from, it could be a lot of things, and I don't think he really knows, either. People always say that you can't blame anybody but yourself, but that's just total bullshit, really, when someone comes out and says that. Truth is: you can blame everybody but yourself. It's the world that did this to you. You are the one killing yourself to cope, not them, and that's why they believe they can get away with saying stupid shit. They think they're stronger than you.

MENTAL

I always figured I'd end up in the nuthouse like my grandma did. I don't really know why, but that's what I always felt. I never met her, but in my mind she's a pretty idea. She died in an asylum, long before I was born, down in Oklahoma, because she refused to eat. She called it fasting, and she starved to death, an act of sacrifice, her final act. Before she died, she suffered intense visitations from angels, telling her of the final days, revealing the truth behind the renewals and damnations of souls, and there was no telling where or when they would pop up to see her. She'd transcribe everything the angels said on a typewriter, hundreds of sheets of the stuff, and conceal them in a tattered brown box beneath her bed. A few years ago, my mom received the box from her aunt. I don't know if she ever read the stuff, she probably doesn't want to, but I know that it's there for her to ponder if she ever accepts the challenge, tucked away now beneath *her* bed, because that is where the angels sleep, the only place that keeps them quiet at night. Sometimes I wonder if there's even a god. Other times I feel this hand that lifts me to a level where I am allowed to hear my dead grandmother's voice.

VIETNAM

My dad's a Vietnam War veteran who smokes two packs a day and works for the United States Postal Service. He works third shift, his secrets seem numerous, and when he's at home he's just a soft squishy surface in front of the television. He watches the news and talks excessively about the "incompetent" leadership in America. He's patriotic, but not grossly so like some dudes. He's never flown the flag all over the front yard, never gotten a license plate made special for Vets, never claimed to be anybody's hero. He is though, a hero, I'll tell you that right now. He used to be an alcoholic, too, before he married my mom and had the idea of creating children. Grandpa was both verbally and physically abusive. The story my mom tells us is that my dad bore the brunt of it, being the oldest of three children. Maybe that's why he's always been so cold and distant. Or was it mostly the war that did that to him? It's really hard to tell sometimes, I know that much. Or maybe it was a combination of everything in his life to a point. My dad caught a bullet in the leg,

I think the left one, when he was over in the jungle, and now he has a funny way about him when he walks. He retired from bowling and golf in his mid-twenties. Sometimes when you wake him up for dinner he'll wake with a start and stare at you as though you were never there at all. And if you ask him about the war, he'll tell you all the things you weren't really asking for. He'll tell you about the time a new guy in the lab did a botch job on a VD test. Apparently how these tests work is, you take a scalpel and heat it red-hot under a flame, then you dip it into sterile water to cool it. After it has sufficiently cooled, you scrape the infected area, put the scrapings under a microscope and look for signs of gonorrhea or herpes or whatever. Well, the new guy forgot the step with the water, the scrapings never made it to the microscope and one good soldier went back to his wife with VD cauterized into his penis under a scalpel-shaped scar. These are the stories he tells us. He doesn't tell us about all the death and destruction he witnessed, the horror and misery, but goes for the lighter stuff, the goofy and reasonable, the stuff that could put a smile on any old face. There's another one, about a guy who caught shrapnel in the ass while shitting in the jungle, and you sit there when the story is done and over (*and then? and then?*) just hoping this will be the day he comes out and says it, comes out with all of it, the more serious stuff, the things the movies are made of, the Rambo shit. But he never does. If you ask my dad about the bullet in his leg, most likely he'll delve into another one of his hilarious VD stories and nothing more. But if you ask him at just the right moment, in the right kind of light, he'll steady his shaky gaze to greet you, head hung like a dusty trophy between his shoulders, and tell you all about the magic bullet that brought him home.

JUST RAIN

He picks me up in the alley in his rusty old pickup. He just sort of grunts when I get in and goes for the gas. I take the hint and stare through the window at the trees. Pretty soon they're little more than a wide green strip pressed against the greying sky.

I say: Cindy says you've been hanging around with Scott.

I say: Looks like maybe some rain.

I say: Why'd you want me to come if you aren't even going to talk to me?

He says: Last night, I saw two fat momma raccoons with seven little babies. I watched them awhile, scavenging around for food. But I got cinder blocks on the garbage cans with bungees strapped across the tops, so they weren't getting anything there.

He laughs, spitting tobacco juice in a Bud Light bottle, one hand on the steering wheel, digging the curves of his crotch with the other.

He says: I saw they were about to give up, so I went inside and dug some scraps of meat out of the trash. And you know what—you know what they did?

I say: What'd they do.

He says: I'll tell you what they did. They tore each other fucking apart.

He spits again, a big ole glob of amber, and turns the radio up a notch—a bunch of fuzz with a preacher's voice bleeding through it.

He says: Those fucking animals.

I say: Always up to something, aren't they?

He says nothing. He's all eyes thrust against a wet windshield and alcohol in his veins.

I say: So you've been hanging around with Scott?

He says: See that cloud swirling up there?

He says: Man, rain's really starting to come down.

I say: Maybe you should slow it down a bit.

The sky is grey, the rain blowing sideways in sheets, and when I look over to inspect the odometer, the needle's stuck at 90.

I say: Pleeeeeeease. Slooooooooow. Dooooooooown.

I say: How can you even fucking see?

He says: You'll be all right. You always are, aren't you?

I say: Just slow the fuck down, okay?

He slows down just a smidge.

I notice some   blood on his shirt, shape of Florida, as a semi passes, all headlights and weight, one unhealthy motherfucker behind the wheel, skulking roadways for something to do come nightfall.

I say: What's on your shirt?

I say: Is that blood on your shirt?

He says: Listen.

He says: I thought I already told you.

He says: I haven't been hanging around with Scott, all right?

I nod and slide down into my seat, lighting a cigarette, alone, hoping the sky changes to pink to orange to light. But the storm only thickens, and a couple times I feel the truck hydroplane beneath me, all four tires skipping over the water like eroded stones—and I don't even know where we're going.

THERAPY

When I was twelve or thirteen my parents made me see a lady, a black woman named Sarah, because they thought I was dangerous. I guess it was true. I was constantly getting into fights, I never fit in with anybody, and when it came to defense, I couldn't control myself once I got started. The thing is: my folks were afraid I'd kill somebody someday. Me? I couldn't kill anybody, not on purpose. I don't know how many times I tried telling them that, but they wouldn't listen. The whole time I was in counseling with this lady I never said a word, except maybe hi and bye. Otherwise I just sat there in silence, a respectful void between us. She was so patient with me. She'd just stare at me and wait until I felt comfortable enough to say something. I never felt comfortable. I went to see her every other week for a few months, and in all that time, we both materialized patience within one another unlike anything I've witnessed since. Even though I never talked to her, or very little, she helped me. I stopped hurting people, stopped fighting back when I was taunted.

I took the abuse and turned it inward. I began hating myself instead of others. Then puberty came on like a plague. I started taking Prozac and listening to music that reflected my feelings through its feedback. I hid further inside myself, deeper in my guts, because I knew it would be nearly impossible for anybody to find me there. I felt comfortable in this sadness, alone, deep down in the void of myself, laid out on top of pitiful pillows in a dirty bedroom, where I never found any kind of useful sleep or even rest from the misery of being me.

INDIAN

My brother's skinny friend, the Seminole who took PCP in my basement the night the redheaded dude showed us his shins, was always coming over late at night, sneaking in with a backpack full of booze, DVDs, CDs, and random magazines, and we'd all sit around drinking and sampling music, watching a mute TV screen full of fucked and flickering images. Movies: David Lynch, Harmony Korine, Werner Herzog, and David Cronenberg. Music videos: Richard Kern, The Nine Inch Nails VHS called Closure. Old Betty Page peep-show shit, a three-disc set, and serial killer documentaries on A&E. We'd listen to Pigface and KMFDM and Nick Cave and Ssab Songs and My Bloody Valentine and Leadbelly and Joy Division. We'd lower our faces and glower, knowing even with all of our combined musical ambitions and artistic visions we could never possibly dream of being so good. Different, yes, but come on, we were dealing with the greats here, weren't we, and we barely had the right kind of equipment to get going on a cover song, let alone an original. Besides, my brother traded my guitar for an eight ball of meth, and he was nearly into his second week of no sleep, concocting ideas for all the songs he would write after he got his hands on another, "cooler" instrument. *What about a bass? Seriously, what if I got a bass?*

~~The last time I thought about death, I thought of you.~~

FOSSILS

I'm in my crib, screaming my little head off. It's dark. Shadows are sneaking in through the window. I'm reaching out from my crib, standing. If I reach any farther, I'll surely fall, but I don't know that, it's only a feeling. I can hear music that sounds spooky, voices that rasp and graze at my ears, little clips of dialogue. My mom peeks in the door, asks me to quiet down: *Just lie back down, sweetie, and go to bed.* The door closes. I stop shouting, but I'm left in the dark, still reaching out, and now the rose bush is scratching against the window. It sounds like a creaky door opening and closing, opening and closing. The shadows look like arms. I can see the dinosaurs on the wallpaper. I imagine them coming to life. I lie down and stare. I stare at the ceiling. And I think: *The dinosaurs are coming to life—they're coming to life.* But I don't think in vocabulary, it's only a feeling. I should be scared. I'm not scared. I start laughing silently. I can't stop. I still hear it. I'm trying to wake the world with it, and I'm not even making a sound, not a peep, it's all inward, hidden away inside of me, a vacuum.

HITLER'S MUSTACHE

Denise hadn't even been at Maize High three months when the rumors began. I was in a mandatory physical education class, second period, the first time I saw her. She was in the class right after mine and we brushed shoulders in the hallway a few times. She was pretty enough, I'd say, with long wood-burnt hair down her back in waves and an olive complexion like a Greek. She was in the middle ground on fashion which told me all I needed to know about her life at home. I was in the same boat myself. My parents never could afford to make me a popular walkabout with their conservative clothing purchases. It's like my dad used to say, *You take what you can get. Then later, when you're all grown-up, you'll thank god you didn't have enough.*

It was after gym when Denise came walking by and tried talking with Joe Donnelly. Joe gave her the cold shoulder and said, *Oh, wait, do I know you?* Quick as machinery Denise sniffed her face into her head, sucked back her tears, washing away the few nice memories of the boy, and wiped her nose on her puke-tan cardigan. She looked suicidal, really. I tried to say something, apologize for Joe, but nothing came to me. *If her head wasn't destined for a noose*, I thought, *it surely is now.* I felt rotten. But her hurt had no effect on Joe. In fact, he just kept walking—strutting, really. He left her in the dust, a backdrop—and, shamefully, so did I.

That was fucked, man. I had to pause a moment, process my guts. *Jesus,* I said, *that's just plain fucked-up, dude.*

Joe laughed. *Yeah*, he said. *It's whatever, man. She's old news. I banged her a week ago, right up against my dad's T-bird. Pretty decent, but I'm through with her now—old news.* He flexed his muscles, had a peek at those few smallish lumps before slinging his letter jacket up and around his shoulders. He laughed. *Dude, that chick doesn't know the first thing about grooming. Now, me, myself, I like it when it's sheared. And usually*, he said, stabbing both thumbs into his chest, *in my experience, these chicks keep it that way, ready. But she doesn't know the first thing about it.* He paused, tightened some curls around his index finger, face puzzled, scrunched and abstracted by memory. *It was like…like…it was like Hitler's mustache or something. I swear to god, dude—I've never seen anything like it,* he said. He shook his head and laughed a cold minute straight. And then he hushed into slow silence when he saw his girlfriend, Blaire Shepherd, crossing over from the bathroom to greet us.

By fifth period a third of the school knew, some of the crueler ones giving the old "Heil Hitler" salute behind Denise's back as she passed them in the halls. All day long her eyes sought after the perpetrators of the laughter and all day the sound abruptly shifted to a fade before her stare could focus and penetrate them.

In Mrs. Jones's class, Earth Science, seventh period, I heard about Denise's mustache from Amelia St. Claire, which was shocking, because Amelia wasn't the type to gossip. She was in all the clubs, including the religious one all the Episcopalians flooded on Tuesday morning. Nothing special, I guess, just shocking, coming from her.

I thought about it a lot, especially that first night. It repulsed me. I mean, I kind of had a crush on the girl for a while and then all the sudden this stuff about a "Hitler mustache" comes about and gets me thinking she's gross.

A few weeks later Mathew Darby wrote on his Twitter feed: *What a night. And yes, it's true. #HeilHitler.*

Turk Van Deeson was the only kid I talked to that year who thought the whole thing with Denise was fucked-up. *Just so typical,* he said. *People can be so fucked-up and stupid. It's like sociopathic behavior or something, almost, if you ask me—all these Dahmer wannabes, these Nazis and pederasts of the fucking future, walking the halls like they own the goddamn century—so fucking typical. They should be counting their prayers, really, you know, if they pray, that she didn't come in here blasting away with her daddy's glock. Really, man—I'm serious as a fucking heart attack. I wouldn't have blamed her, if she had. Alright, maybe that's a little dramatic. But what do I care? My conscience is clean.*

He searched his backpack for a lighter, came up empty-handed, then looked around the school parking lot to make sure we weren't being watched.

You got a light?

Sorry. I don't smoke, I said, lying.

He looked at me with those strange burning eyes of his.

Really, I told him, *I don't.*

He hissed, called me a *fucking liar,* spat on the sidewalk, and wiped his hand, with this penned-on skull near his knuckles, through a greasy clump of green hair.

All of this eventually culminated in me asking Denise to the homecoming dance after P.E. one day. I crossed my fingers and scrunched my face. I worried she'd notice the yellow pit-stains on my T-shirt, that I hadn't showered with the jocks in the locker room because I was too scared of their manlier physiques and abundant pubic populations, but she didn't care about all that, and, to my surprise, she said yes, and with no reluctance of voice either—just pure sweetness, a voice like candy. She had this big smile across her face and her skin looked made out of only the best things of the earth.

My mom dropped us off at the school at 8:00.

By 8:15 we were ten blocks away, at Sunrise Park, fooling around by the seesaw.

By 8:20 my fingers were lost inside her, my mouth wet and tugging at her lips and tongue, latching to her teeth and sucking in her breath by the lungful.

It's true, by the way, what they said about her pubic foliage, the historical horizontal shape, and I took it all in, too, all I could swallow of it—and it was beautiful and righteous and everything that hadn't been said or taught or even permitted of me to think.

We never talked to each other again.

Every time I think of Denise, my heart gurgles. I didn't understand it for the longest time. But I think sometimes truth can only come out as gurgles, and most of the time, that's the only way it makes any sense. Sounds like a heart with holes, taking on water. The truth of my story is my heart was already fucked and sinking, long before the rumors even began. It's not an excuse, it's a fact.

I think I'm in love.

What if the diviner tells us that when he holds the rod he *feels* that the water is five feet under the ground? or that he *feels* that a mixture of copper and gold is five feet under the ground? Suppose that to our doubts he answered: "You can estimate a length when you see it. Why shouldn't I have a different way of estimating it?"

—Ludwig Wittgenstein

BLACK FRIEND

The only black friend I had growing up was a guy who could skateboard better than anybody I'd ever seen. I envied him. For a brief time, he was a hero of mine. Another kid I used to skate with called him a "nigger" one day, face to face under the shade of a maple. *Dude's a nigger with white nipples,* he said. It was crazy. I froze where I was, back against bark and with my heart all choked up into my throat like a fist, waiting for the violence to come on like a warm blanket of phlegm. But my black friend only smirked and moved away from the tree branches, laughing. He could've killed the kid if he'd wanted to. Apparently he wanted for deeper things. He wanted the things in being you can never even come close to touching—the things there are no words for.

10 ALBUMS

1. *My Bloody Valentine* (self-titled)

2. John Fahey's *Death Chants, Breakdowns, and Military Waltzes*

3. Joy Division's *Unknown Pleasures*

4. *Under the Pink*—Tori Amos

5. Leonard Cohen's *Songs of Love and Hate*

6. *Here Come the Warm Jets*—Brian Eno

7. Bowie's *Diamond Dogs*

8. The Cure's *Disintegration*

9. Tupac Shakur's *Strictly 4 My N.I.G.G.A.Z.*

10. *Moonpix*—Cat Power

YOU'VE GOT IT: THAT MODEL LOOK, LIKE IN THE KLEIN ADS

Hey Bro,

When you're on meth you get to looking like a hag in no time. Pretty soon you start terrorizing your family with thefts. Threatening phone calls slice through the wires almost every other day. Sometimes you chew your fingernails down to where they nearly bleed and, when there's nothing left, you start chewing pens and DVD cases and cigarette cartons and toenails. You spit the bits all over the floor. One time you got pistol-whipped and punched in the nose. You pick at your face and wonder why you're ugly. Sometimes you masturbate for hours, so desensitized to your own touch that you wouldn't feel a needle tunneling the canals of your urethra, too busy jostling the shriveled thing in your fist to even notice, watching outsized twat flutter on the television screen like some kind of obscene butterfly fading into light. Your bedroom smells like a mildewed shoehorn, or ass, I can't really tell the difference. If I didn't love you so much, I wouldn't tell you this, but when you came back home after months of street-life, the way you looked actually made my stomach feel all kinds of fucked-up. I don't know if I was disgusted or relieved, but you looked like a skeleton vacuum-packed in cellophane, ready to strike a pose beneath any ghetto streetlight. I wanted to thrust a bucket of lard at you and hand you a spoon. I wanted you to have something thick and meaty around your bones so you'd never get cold at night. It was striking, the way your tiny arms shivered. I thought the streets had killed you. Yet there you were, sifting through me like an apparitional thing. I thought about reaching over and searching your wrist for a pulse, anything, mud, but I pulled back. I just couldn't do it. I didn't want to see the look on your face when I told myself the news.

Love always and forever,

Your Baby Brother

P.S. Please don't tell Mom I was with you.

THE DEAD FISHERMAN

We found a dead fisherman at the lake. He was sitting with his head thrown back, fishing pole held tight and upright in his hands. His skin was red and flaky from sun exposure. I couldn't tell if it was him or the lake that smelled like shit. We circled around him like flies, observing the stillness of his body. Then I saw a finger move. Well, it didn't really move, just kind of vibrated. Then I realized the pole was moving, not his finger, and I tried to pry his fingers apart to get the pole free but couldn't even budge them. I looked out and watched the bobber go all the way under, the pole arching with the weight of the fish. I tried to get to the pole again. My friends wanted to leave. *Dude, let's get the fuck out of here. C'mon, man. Let's go.* I didn't want to leave. I said, *Hold it. Just hang on a minute.* I wanted to see if the fish would free itself, but the bobber never came back up, and we left the dead fisherman there, all alone, to reel it home.

The last time I thought about death, it was only a dream.

MIDGET

I went ice skating with a midget once. Not a real midget, just this kid I knew who suffered from some kind of full-body deformity, more like Simon Birch than Wee Man, and he wore these amazing glasses that made his eyes look swollen huge in his tiny head. He was only about three feet tall. He lived in a trailer park and smoked pot. I went to his birthday party in eighth grade. Everybody was getting high while scoping the junkyard. He had a rattail that fell down his back like dirty curling ribbon. His chest was all puffed out, a bowling ball berthed under his ribcage. I remember hearing Kid Rock float out from his trailer and into the driveway. He always seemed to be smiling, weasel-like laughter frothing from his crooked teeth, when he wasn't putting on a mean face to look tough. He presented himself as the type of badass figure you might find in a novel by S.E. Hinton. His birthday party is seared into my brain. I think he only made it to one or two more. Later that year, they did full-body surgeries on him, breaking and resetting bones, trying to stretch him out with machines and braces so that he might be a little taller someday. They succeeded in making him just shy of four inches taller, and he seemed to be on top of the world for a while, showing off his newest strut and stature, finally feeling that sense of equality with his fellow boy that he'd always yearned for. But he only lasted another year. He wasn't meant for the tall life. It was those extra few inches that killed him.

SUICIDE

The first was early sophomore year and I didn't really know the guy that well. I only knew that he was nice, and that everybody loved him. At the funeral, everyone wore yellow windbreaker pants and jackets in honor of his choice of Halloween costume the previous year: a Chiquita banana. Guess it was a real hit.

The second was just a little after the first. But it was a girl this time, a girl I actually kind of knew a little, an acquaintance I'd talked to a few times during lunch. We were just getting to know each other. She always seemed sad even when she was cheerful. She hung herself from her ceiling fan. At least that's what I was told.

The third was a kid I knew pretty well. I'd skated with him a few times around town, and we had Technology class together during third block. One day he just stopped coming to class. A few weeks later somebody explained to me what had happened. He used a gun. I'd been under the assumption he had transferred to another school.

The fourth wasn't suicide per se: dude did too many drugs, drank too much alcohol, passed out at a party and never woke up. His funeral drew more people than the previous three combined. I guess his suicide was accidental, unlike the others, so his funeral boasted a more apologetic feel.

I got really paranoid and lazy with life. I dropped out of school, thinking there was something contagious there. Who knows, maybe I'd be the next one to go. Of course I wasn't, but you can never get that kind of stench off you. People kill themselves all the time, in every country, on every fucking continent I in the world. They don't feel any guilt about it. Why should they? They leave that behind for the living. I feel guilty all the time.

they were the best of times, they were the worst of times, they were the

best of times, they were the worst of times, they were the best of times,

they were the worst of times, they were the best of times, they were the

worst of times, they were the best of times, they were the worst of times,

they were the best of times, they were the worst of times, they were the

best of times, they were the worst of times, they were the best of times,

they were the worst of times, they were the best of times, they were the

worst of times, they were the best of times, they were the worst of times,

they were the best of times, they were the worst of times, they were the

best of times, they were the worst of times, they were the best of times,

they were the worst of times, they were the best of times, they were the

worst of times, they were the best of times, they were the worst of times,

they were the best of times, they were the worst of times, they were the

best of times, they were the worst of times, they were the best of times,

they were the worst of times, they were the best of times, they were the

worst of times, they were the best of times, they were the worst of times,

they were the best of times, they were the worst of times, they were the

best of times, they were the worst of times, they were the best of times,

they were the worst of times, they were the best of times, they were the

worst of times, they were the best of times, they were the worst of times,

they were the best of times, they were the worst of times, they were the best of times, they were the worst of times, they were the best of times, they were the worst of times, they were the best of times, they were the worst of times, they were the best of times, they were the worst of times, they were the best of times, they were the worst of times, they were the best of times, they were the worst of times, they were the best of times, they were the worst of times, they were the best of times, they were the worst of times, they were the best of times, they were the worst of times, they were the best of times, they were the worst of times, they were the best of times, they were the worst of times, they were the best of times, they were the worst of times, they were the best of times, they were the worst of times, they were told.

ZOMBIE

Here comes the walking dead, one of my ex-best friends, freshman year of high school, cutting his wrists over girls who never loved him, no matter how hard he tried. With the pools of blood on the linoleum, the white bandages with the rose-petal patterns, the ambulance rides the one or two times he came too close, all those weeks spent in hospitals for observation, the Velcro shoes and the five-o'clock shadows, he never even came close to getting what he wanted from these girls. He wanted a companion, a force of two as one, a tenth-grade bride—no traitors allowed. He'd haunt your days with scars, reminding you of your betrayal, if you ever left him. He wanted you for life, something to stuff and put over his mantel, into his head, a laurel, a trophy, a model of your car, the last thing you touched, the one he followed home in his fantasies, driven into his heart with the sharp point of obsession. It wasn't about love with him, really, nor sex. I think more than anything all he ever wanted was a little piece of a life he could try-on, lace-up, and call his own, even if it wasn't and never would be that simple. Resistance was the only common ground between what he really wanted and what he wanted even more. One time I asked him to go ahead and tell what's wrong, because I could tell that something was wrong, you could see it in the shadows under his eyes, but he just stood there blank-faced, mouth hung like a trapdoor, a hole full of dirty tiles in pink mud, and nodded. He couldn't control his lips, just as he couldn't control those girls and their bodies, and they quivered, his breath carving sculptures of everything he'd ever felt, seen, remembered, and dreamed into the folds of the wind. All he had to do was breathe.

READING INTO THINGS

My intro to serious literature, sixteen years old and freshly dropped-out of high school, was *The Picture of Dorian Gray*. It was fine, I liked it okay, and then I forgot about it like it never happened. A few weeks later, I sat down to watch TV with my dad. I was disappointed with his choice, totally bored, and wanted to turn the channel. But then my mind snapped into place, focused in, and I was fully taken in by a young, attractive Angela Lansbury. She mesmerized me. It was the movie adaptation of Wilde's book, the old black and white one, and of course Lansbury was striking in every human way. She looked so pretty and innocent, but at the same time she looked as though she'd lived, had understood the hard times in life and come out the other end. I watched the whole thing, no commercial breaks, from start to finish, didn't even take a breather to piss or sneak a cigarette in the upstairs bathroom.

I thought about her a lot after that, especially at night while I was trying to become a writer. A few months later, I bought a book of poems by Jim Carroll. To my surprise, there was a poem in there that said something about Angela Lansbury sneezing under the ocean, signaling the whales or some sap-shit like that. I can't tell you why, but I thought it was one of the greatest things I'd ever read, at the time, and thought about her even more after that. She visited my room at night, an obsession. I thought about how my mom used to watch *Murder, She Wrote* and bite her fingernails into nubs, just shy of literally sitting on the edge of her seat, when I was a child, and how the old woman on the TV was the same person I'd once thought about sexually as a teenager. They weren't even the same person anymore. The older version was even better.

VACATION

Arkansas in late July is like being wrapped in cellophane and stuffed inside a tanning bed. We are staying in a cabin near Beaver Lake. Everybody is swimming down at the pool, but I stayed behind to give my muscles and skin a rest after a long day of canoeing on the White River. I have burns all up my legs and down my arms. My face looks raw. I'm out on the deck, drinking a can of orange soda and eating chips. It's getting dark, but it's hard to tell because it's always darker in the woods. The branches creak in the heat. I'm waiting for a creature to come out of hiding and be discovered. Nothing comes. Thirty minutes later, still nothing. Sometimes nature cheats you in that way. There are plenty of bugs though—spiders the size of the palm of your hand and flies as big as jelly beans. The bugs are thick, like walls. I get to thinking about things, while watching these bug-clusters, and I'm still thinking about them now. I'm thinking about all the things my life accumulated to a certain point. Let's say the point right before I met my wife. All before her, all of it, seems like just a bunch of shit I can throw out there and tell for the sake of telling and at the same time it's all so much more than that. I'd like to say that none of it matters, but these are the things I had to experience to experience myself as me in the now. Throwing them out with such carelessness would be like pimping out my past on Maury, but forgetting, that would be even worse, like keeping my skin on a coat hanger after pawning my bones for a few scraps of meat.

TWENTY-FIVE BOOKS

1. *Crime and Punishment*—Dostoevsky

2. *Nausea*—Sartre

3. *Ham on Rye*—Bukowski

4. *Green Eggs and Ham*—Seuss

5. *The Journal of Albion Moonlight*—Patchen

6. *The Loser*—Bernhard

7. *The Snows of Kilimanjaro and Other Stories*—Hemingway

8. *The Easter Parade*—Yates

9. *Enormous Changes at the Last Minute*—Paley

10. *The Lover*—Duras

11. *Malone Dies*—Beckett

12. *The Catcher in the Rye*—Salinger

13. *The Immoralist*—Gide

14. *Cannery Row*—Steinbeck

15. *Tropic of Cancer*—Miller

16. *Wise Blood*—O'Connor

17. *The Stranger*—Camus

18. *Anti-Oedipus*—Deleuze and Guattari

19. *The Satyricon*—Petronius

20. *The Passion According to G.H.*—Lispector

21. *Miss Lonely Hearts*—West

22. *The Sickness unto Death*—Kierkegaard

23. *Airships*—Hannah

24. *Closer*—Cooper

25. *Ficciones*—Borges

ad astra per aspera

SISTER, SISTER, SISTER

My sister's seventeen and dating a guy with a pitchfork tattooed on his chest. He has blue eyes and prep-length dirty-blonde hair, plays the guitar, mostly old hair-band rock from the eighties, and looks a little like a child molester with that little tuft of hair above his upper lip. He smokes Marlboros and plays the occasional game of pool. I went with him and my sis to the Bingo Palace one night. An old lady with curlers won the first round. As for the second, I wouldn't know; we left before they even started, and when we got in the car, I could smell liquor on someone's breath. Whether it was hers or his, I'll never know. But this boyfriend of my sister's, he's in his twenties. She met him in rehab. Now she's six months pregnant, working at Sonic, and driving around town in an old Chrysler New Yorker. He's a junkie, alcoholic, and soon-to-be father who works at the Casey's General Store out in Maize. Everybody is really scared about what the future holds for them, my sister and her beau, especially my parents, but I'm happy about the news. I don't understand what all the fuss is about. There'll always be time to worry, won't there? Can't we do that later? But damn it, I'm worrying now—and it *is* later. The baby was born seventeen years ago. The baby's in high school now. He'll be driving soon. In just a few short years he'll outgrow me. He'll be a better man than me. He'll open my eyes, pour in the 3D pinks and blues, and show me how he turned out is all the ways I should've been.

GUNS

I crawl into the strangeness of some books and movies just to feel something familiar, something normal. I leave my fiancé's house to go to my apartment. It's one o'clock in the morning. I'm driving a piece-of-shit Dodge Diplomat, a relic of the eighties. It's the color of taco meat. It's only about six miles home, but three miles in, the halfway point, I pull around the car in front of me, into the center lane, and stop at the red light. I feel like an ass for tailgating the guy, but I'm a nervous person, so I do what anybody would do and look over. Our eyes lock. A gun points at me through an open window. I press hard on the gas and peel through the light.

Did I learn anything?

No.

Has tailgating ever warranted a death?

The world is full of possibilities.

At any rate, when I got home I read the rest of *Funeral Rites* by Jean Genet and took a shower. I couldn't decide which was better: *I'm lucky I'm still alive* or *that should have been it.*

DUMB JOKES I HEARD OVER THE YEARS IN WICHITA

(Age thirteen)

Q: What's the difference between a large pizza and a black man?

A: Large pizza can feed a family of five.

(Age sixteen)

Q: What's more enjoyable than stapling a dead baby to the wall?

A: Tearing it off.

(Age eight)

A: Knock, knock!

Q: Who's there?

A: Little Boy Blue.

Q: Little Boy Blue who?

A: Michael Jackson.

MASTURBATION

My brother pulled his dick out in front of me. It was hard. He tried folding it in half, then realized it hurt and tried an up and down stroke instead. When he discovered he liked that, he didn't stop, wouldn't stop—would never stop. As soon as I left the room, I thought that that looked like a fun thing to do too, so I went into my bedroom and gave it a try. I started out, limper than all hell, by making shapes with it—a circle, a crescent moon—and then I made it serpent-like, thought it looked like the Loch Ness monster. I was scared, though, doing it. My heart pounded so hard it felt like there was a small animal in there trying to eat its way through my solar plexus. Then, slowly, the fear turned into excitement, turned into joy. And after a few proper tugs, when things started to harden up, I feared I too would never stop doing it. And I didn't. A year or two later, I ejaculated all over the carpet, my first orgasm. For two whole years I'd been stopping just short. I looked down at the mess on the carpet, my butthole in a knot, and yanked my jeans up around my hips, feeling accomplished. There was a dirty towel in the laundry basket, which I used to clean up the mess. Then it came, out of nowhere, all these feelings I hadn't really felt before—not that intensely anyway. I felt guilty, I guess, for feeling so good, like I didn't deserve it or something, even though, deep down, I knew that I'd earned it. I mean, I was sweating like a gross-ass pig spun on a spit for days and my arm, Charlie-horsed through and through, was like a dead otter sewn onto my shoulder. There was guilt and shame swimming their circles inside me, but I convinced myself that they were just a couple of stupid little feelings that I would have to learn to live with. If only everybody in the world did the tug-pull and the rub-rub, and all at once, every single one of us, slow and synchronized, guilt-free, then we would finally have some sense of a peaceful world—and possibly, however momentarily, we would feel ourselves free from the shame of living.

WHAT I TALK ABOUT
WHEN I TALK ABOUT
JOYLAND

The time K and I rode the roller coaster and he took the seatbelt off and I was afraid he was going to die.

The time I kissed a girl on that white train that went back into the wooded area and down near the go-cart track.

The time I rode the Log Jam, got a nosebleed, and started to cry.

The time the guy on the lawn crew was mowing the ground under the roller coaster before the park opened for the day and then stuck his head through the slats at the wrong moment and got his head cut off by the roller coaster car coming down the main hill on a practice run—reading about it in the newspaper.

The time the park closed one last time, and we all silently wept.

I saw pictures of Joyland online, with the tagline, "Creepy Abandoned Amusement Park," and I swear, I swear it, that was the last time I ever even looked.

WATER SLIDES

There was this friend of mine who went into the bathroom after this other kid's birthday party and slit both of his wrists. I was sixteen years old, the other two kids were fifteen, and the suicide-attempter was eighteen. It was two o'clock in the morning when it happened. We had been watching movies when he disappeared. The movie ended and he was still in the bathroom. That's when we started to worry. We knocked and knocked and knocked. He didn't respond. We knocked again, quietly saying his name through the door. No response. Alarmed, we took a coat hanger, bent it out of shape, and picked the lock with it. It only took a minute to work the lock and when we got the door open we found him, conscious, standing, watching his blood make small pools on the linoleum floor. There was panic in our hearts, but we were also fairly used to his behavior—we knew what to expect. We wrapped up his wounds the best we could, scotch-taping toilet paper around his wrists. But the tape kept falling off because he was bleeding through it.

So we got into his car and drove to the 24-hour Walmart a few blocks away to get some supplies. It was a still, summer night. The stars were out, a cloudless sky, moon full and shining. When we got to Walmart, we came upon this aerosol stuff in the bandage aisle, a spray that seals up wounds (some kind of strange skin glue), also some butterfly tape, some gauze, and some duct tape, and went back to his house to get our nurse on. We were quiet getting back into the house, trying not to wake anybody, and then we made our way into the downstairs bathroom. It took some time but eventually we got him all fixed up, somehow stopped the bleeding. Luckily he hadn't cut deep enough to rake a vein. By the time we were done with his damaged wrists, it was already closing in on five in the morning. We were going to caravan to Oklahoma City with our friend's parents early that morning, part of the celebration, to spend the day at a water park. *We'll just be more tired if we only sleep two hours.* We said that aloud a few times to convince ourselves of its staying power but knew it was a bad idea before our lips even moved. All we knew was that we were going to spend the day at a water park. We were going to smile. We had a two-hour drive ahead of us, a few packs of cigarettes and some weed to smoke. We made sure the slits in his wrists were watertight. We were not about to let anything get in our way. We were going to go shoot down some water slides.

THRESHOLD DANCES

Growing up, I'd heard about this guy—the serial killer who got away—but we didn't talk about him much. I think people who were alive during the murders didn't like to think about it. My mom and dad lived through it, as it was happening, and have relayed that it was definitely a pretty scary time around here. This guy damn near took out a whole family, the Oteros, not even counting the others. Jerking-off on his victim's corpses and taking pictures of them in various poses, he sent letters into news stations and the police chief, tauntingly, with cryptic messages and clues, and nobody could catch him. By the time I was old enough to know anything about it, years had passed since he had actually killed somebody. So many years, in fact, that most people assumed he was in a different state, or dead, or for some reason or other unable to kill again—everybody had their theories.

2004. It was on every news station, in all the papers. He was back. In fact, he had never even left us. Leaving clues around the city again, too—at Home Depot (a cereal box containing a letter and trophies from his victims), *The Wichita Eagle* (a letter from one Bill Thomas Killman, a few postcards, etc., all detailing his crimes in grotesque detail), KAKE News (postcards detailing crimes, giving clues, toying around), off the highway up near Park City (another cereal box, this one containing a bound doll, apparently symbolizing the death of an eleven-year-old girl he'd killed). I remember a word puzzle he sent the cops. They published it in *The Wichita Eagle* hoping somebody would decipher the code or recognize his handwriting. I had a blast trying to solve that thing. I thought I'd crack it, help them put that creep behind bars, but it was clearly just a box of random unsolvable gibberish. I mean, the FBI couldn't even crack it. It was evident that he liked the attention. It was also evident, if the case went cold, as it had in the past, he'd have one sad killer heart inside him, because that's what really got him off, the attention—and nobody wanted that. No, he would undoubtedly kill again, if they didn't catch him sooner or later. That's the way they left it, the news coverage acting as an incubator for our fears. We were left with a sick feeling when we went outside at night. We'd hesitate in the thresholds of doors, do a little dance there. Our hearts pumped a glaze of adrenaline over the linings of our veins. I know it's fucked up, but it was one of the most exciting times in my life. It made me feel alive again—and in a way that was healthy.

His name had been BTK for so long that when he slipped up and they caught him, I was disappointed to hear his real name was Dennis Rader. To me, he just didn't look like a Dennis. But he sure didn't look like a Richard or a John Wayne or a Charles, either. He just looked like a guy who got up every morning, went to his job, came home to his wife in the evenings, and went to worship his god in a church on Sunday.

And guess what?

That's exactly who he was.

TRANSVESTITE

My dad took me and my friend to the flea market one weekend when we were nine. This was back when you could still smoke cigarettes in public places. So we were in the food court eating chili dogs and my dad was smoking his cigarettes and drinking a cup of coffee. We were into coin collecting, all three of us, so we were looking at our wheat pennies and our buffalo nickels. Then, out of nowhere, my friend started blushing, eyes fixed to his plate, very clearly distraught, so my dad asked him: *What's the problem?* And my friend, he said: *That lady looks like an old man,* pointing his finger. My dad couldn't hold his laughter. He doubled over the newspaper he was staring at, and when he finished laughing, he patted my friend on his back and said: *That lady looks like an old man because she is an old man.* Both of us were taken off guard. *Why'd he dress like that?* My dad laughed again, stubbing his cigarette out in the ashtray, and whispered loudly: *He's a fairy. That's what he's into.*

And then I wondered if that's what I was into. I thought of all the times my older sister put makeup on me. I thought about all the times I'd ever played with Barbie dolls of my own free will. I thought about what my friends might think of me, if they knew I enjoyed it when my sister let me play with her girly toys. I wondered what it would be like to be a man dressed as a woman, especially in a world so clearly dominated by men who dressed like men.

SUICIDES (A LIST):

Ian Curtis (hanging)

Ernest Hemingway (gunshot)

Breece D'J Pancake (gunshot)

Kurt Cobain (gunshot)

Albert Ayler (drowning)

Hart Crane (drowning)

Ann Quin (drowning)

Jerzy Kosinski (asphyxiation: plastic bag)

Vincent Van Gogh (gunshot)

Sylvia Plath (asphyxiation: gas)

Mark Rothko (slit wrists)

Anne Sexton (asphyxiation: carbon monoxide, *The Awful Rowing Toward God*)

Virginia Woolf (drowning)

A CAT DIES

At three years old, with a thick mass of curly hair and a smile that could break your heart in half, my brother shoved his pet cat into the freezer and shut the door. He was watching his favorite TV show and she was fucking everything up because she kept scratching at the screen. The cat fucking died. No one really knows how long she was in there. Long enough to shit everywhere and freeze solid. Long enough for her soul to get out into the air, enter my father's scrotum and mix with his seed. I was born a year later. Every time I think of my brother I find it difficult to breathe.

BAPTISMS FOR THE DEAD

We took a bus down to Dallas, TX, probably forty or fifty of us, and spent the night praying for our families in a large hotel room. The next morning we drove to the temple. We had to change into all-white clothes when we got inside. There was a large dressing room. Old men of no relation changed their clothes next to teenage boys, not even attempting modesty. We filed into a big room. The light was dim. We all sat in pews, observing the baptisms as they progressed. They went on and on well into the afternoon.

The baptismal was a large basin, about fifteen feet in diameter, elevated atop statues of oxen. Everything was white. Nothing was pure. As soon as I got into the basin and the water hit the shriveled thing I call my penis, I peed my pants. I didn't feel too bad about it, either, like I thought I would. Then this guy read a few things about the lives of the dead—a few Jews, some Catholics, a crippled agnostic. He dunked me under the water each time he read a new name. It went on like this forever. When I finally got out, I felt like shit. I had water in my nose, inside my sinuses, and bad thoughts all shot through my head. But there I was, the obedient Mormon, newly baptized for twenty poor, dead, non-Mormon souls. *Finally,* somebody said, *these people have been elevated to the gates of heaven.*

Amen.

On the bus back to Wichita something in me clicked. I experienced the mind-numbing madness of depression for the first time in my life. And later that night, after getting home and telling my parents how great the trip had been, I crawled up into my bed and pulled the covers over my head, prayer-less, and fell asleep. It was a conscious decision I made, not praying, not even going through the motions. I just didn't feel like doing it anymore, not even for the souls of the living. I didn't feel like doing anything. But I couldn't stop thinking about things. As I lay there, all cocooned in my bedspread, I couldn't stop, my mind reeling through thousands of memories, thoughts, questions and questions and questions, all rapid-fire and all at once. *God? God? Are you there, God? Are you listening?*

RACIST BILL

My buddies used to buy weed from a guy who had a Confederate flag draped across the wall in his living room and a stuffed monkey hanging from a noose in his entryway. They called him Racist Bill. He wore tank tops and cowboy boots and spit his tobacco spit into empty Bud Light cans. I personally never met Bill, but I listened to their stories with quite a bit of interest, especially the one about the time they took our friend A. J. over to buy some weed. A.J. was six feet five inches tall, about three hundred pounds, and he happened to be half-black, too. Bill wasn't so big and bad anymore, with A.J. around. He took him into his home without a word. In fact, he laughed when A.J. made fun of some of the items he saw laying around his house. *What the fuck is that? Ah—man, why would you want to hang a monkey? What do you have against monkeys?*

Bill shrugged, face red, a bit of nervous laughter, and said, *Guess I just thought it was funny.*

THE YAK-YAK GIRL

This girl I knew in eighth grade had the hugest crush on me and wouldn't stop talking to me whenever I saw her. Sounds nice, but it was actually a big problem for me. I was unapologetically in love with her best friend, who wasn't in love with me, and I made no bones about it. This Yak-Yak Girl's enthusiasm really pissed me off. She'd come up to me in the morning near the vending machines, and in the halls during passing period, and outside near the busses at the end of the school day, suffocating me with her I♥U sign language and bear hugs. It was like being waterboarded. Not to be a dick, but I wasn't that into her. Every single place I went—*poof*—she'd be there too. She'd just come along and start talking about the stupidest shit, messing with my musical tastes and personal flavor. She'd yak-yak my fucking ears straight off if I let her.

And then my birthday came. I had to invite this yak-yak girl, otherwise the girl I liked wouldn't come. At my party she tried to kiss me. I pushed her away and said: *Eww. I don't want you. I want her,* and I pointed a finger toward the girl of my immediate obsessions, who happened to be right there, standing in my best friend's backyard, sneaking a cigarette. And the girl I wanted, the one who I was painfully in love with, she gave me what I thought I needed—out of pity. We made out for a good twenty minutes, and the whole time, I thought: *I love you, I love you, I love you.* But I could hear the Yak-Yak Girl crying during all of this, one of my friends over with her on the porch trying to tell her *it just wasn't meant to be, you know.* When it was all said and done and the night was over, I started crying, too. I lay there, on the floor, drunk and alone, my eyes stinging, cheeks red, thinking out loud in the hoarsest of whispers: *Next year we'll all be in high school. This kind of shit happens all the time in high school. These are the moments that lives are made of.*

SONGS BY TORI AMOS
(IN NO PARTICULAR ORDER)

1. "Putting the Damage On"

2. "Silent all these Years"

3. "Winter"

4. "Cornflake Girl"

5. "Pretty Good Year"

6. "Mr. Zebra"

7. "Icicle"

8. "Crucify"

9. "Little Earthquakes"

10. "Leather"

RICH KIDS

A few years after high school, this rich kid I knew got really fucked up, started looking like a clone of himself, only thirty years older and dead in the eyes. Meth. Turns out he did some time in jail. Like I said, he was rich, but apparently, even though he was back living at home, mommy and daddy had cut him off financially and he found himself out of dope one night when they were out of the country on vacation. Out of money, too, and probably going through the first throngs of withdrawal. So he tried to find a way around that. Instead of doing what my brother did and stealing from his own family, he did the respectable thing. He decided he'd call in a pizza. Pepperoni, cheese, supreme, doesn't matter—he didn't give a shit about the pizza.

When the pizza delivery guy got to his front door, this rich kid, he pulled one of his daddy's guns on the poor man, robbed him blind. Surely didn't make off with much. But the kicker, the thing that gets me going is, he went and got the drugs and then returned to the scene of the crime to do them. So when the cops came banging on the door of his parent's mansion, he thought he'd just be able to talk his way out of it. *It's that poor immigrant's word over mine,* he probably thought, as the rich often do. Wrong. He got locked up for quite a while.

I saw him at the gas station the other day. Nothing has changed. People who use, you can spot them a mile away. His skin looked like ancient, tattooed parchment, teeth all rotten, and he only put two dollars' worth of unleaded into his car so that he could get to wherever it was he was going. I felt his defeat seep into me. Driving away, I kept thinking, *I should have said hello. I should have said hello.* So I pulled around, drove back into the gas stall and cut the engine. He was just sitting in his car, rolling a cigarette or a joint, I wasn't sure which, and listening to Mariah Carey on the FM dial. I walked up and knocked.

He rolled down the window. *Who the fuck are you?*

Troy, I said. *Troy Weaver. We went to school together. Maize High School.*

He looked at me with this blank expression—he didn't remember me—and then he said, *Yeah, I remember you.* It was a cigarette he was rolling. He lit it, blew the blue smoke through his nose like an untamed bull. *I have to go.* Then he turned the radio up even louder. *It was nice seeing you,* he hollered, and drove off. I just stood there for a minute, thinking, *I should have just said hello.*

REVISION I

Turns out my grandmother didn't die in the mental hospital. She spent some time in a mental hospital, but didn't die there. She was treated for paranoid schizophrenia. They would strap her in and shock her into not hearing voices anymore, at least for a while. The reality is she died in a Salvation Army homeless shelter. Fasting remains her cause of death. And here I thought, all this time, that fasting was supposed to be a good thing, a holy thing, something that gets you step by step and inch by inch closer to god. I don't know—I don't believe it anymore. Suffering is still suffering. I don't find any virtue in it. So, tell me, who was it? Who was there to save her from the voices in her head? Other voices, I suppose—voices named after angels. Well, they found their purchase, didn't they, the fuckers.

REVISION II

The midget of my middle school years, the one I thought had died after his numerous surgeries, with his rat tail and his huge prescription glasses, is still alive. Imagine, all this time I believed he was dead. Apparently, what really happened is, he just never came back to school. He was home schooled. And then the rumors happened. I'd heard from somebody that he died, believed them, and even briefly mourned his death. I've spent all these years thinking he was at home with the worms and ghostly in the night, stalking behind headstones and scaring groundskeepers.

Thinking back, I realize how strange it is that I never heard a single word about his funeral. No, he's a rapper now—goes by the name of Salty Faulty—and he'll outlive the upcoming dust crops and global warming and bomb blasts so long as these words are not burned from this page. God made him ugly to elevate him above us. I mean, I'm sure through all these years that have quietly passed between us he has never even once thought to himself about *my* death. No, he's better than that. He's probably the type of person who puts absolutely no stock in rumors, however true they must be.

DATE RAPE

I used to hang out with this guy a couple years older than me. We rode the school bus together from fifth grade all the way up to ninth, maybe even tenth grade, and then, when we were out of school, both failures, never having made it to college or even a good job, all we really ever did was get drunk with our friends and try scoring with the ladies.

But mostly we drank.

He was renting this house with two or three other dudes in one of the historic parts of town, with its old houses, huge trees, and rickety power lines, and all we did day after day was soak our livers in Bud Light and whiskey, from noon until we fell asleep there at night, the smell of sweat, puke, and asshole never quite distant enough for comfort.

Though the women were few and far between, there was the occasional party girl that would swing by to visit one of the guys. Not me, though,

I usually took a back seat to such endeavors. I used to tell myself that it was because I had more respect for women than those guys, but I'm afraid I was lying to myself. I was just too shy to ever try to get up in a girl's skirt, let alone unbuckle her pants.

One night we helped this girl down the street move her things into a big U-Haul—she was moving to Kansas City to live with her fiancée—and in return for our help she bought us a couple of cases of beer and some pizzas.

We all got blasted playing beer pong.

It was late and people were dropping off like flies. In fact, I think I was the first one out—down for the count on one of the two couches in the living room, using three or four books under my head as a pillow even though the real pillow was right there on the floor not even two feet away. My shoes were still on. My eyes were closed. My body was spinning. I felt like puking but kept my throat tight, forcing it all back into me, and when the roller coaster ride was over, I fell asleep tucked into a ball.

I couldn't tell if it was a dream or not, but I heard a girl panting, flesh smacking flesh. I opened my eyes. It was dark, completely dark, and

I couldn't see anything, even after my eyes had adjusted, so I just lay there and listened.

Then I heard a girl's voice: *You have to stop. It hurts.* And then: *Stop it. Please, stop it.*

It wasn't a dream, but I was too drunk to stand, too sick from drink, but I tried to say something, anything, but it came out all muffled and slurred and half-thought in the first place.

Shut the fuck up!

I did, I did shut the fuck up, and then crawled back into my hall of silence, but I could still hear the flesh on flesh, maybe five minutes of it, progressing with each second into a pounding muddle of sound. She kept saying: *It hurts. Please stop.* And his response was: *I'm almost done. Seriously, hush, I'm almost done. Doesn't it feel good? It feels good, doesn't it? Fuck, just stop moving like that, I'm almost done. Seriously, give me a minute.* And she kept saying: *Stop. Please. Stop it, I'm too dry,* but he didn't listen, this friend of mine, nobody listened, and I never said a thing about it, not to anybody, until now. But what else can I say or do to make anybody feel better about this? How can I take away the pain and help heal any wounds?

I'll say this: I'm sorry beyond words, I've never felt more ashamed, but when the time comes, and I hope it does, I hope this "friend" feels all the pain, and all the shame, that he's created.

WHERE IS MY MIND

A few years back, I read in the local newspaper that one of my brother's friends, the one with red hair who infamously jammed a nail into his shin with a claw hammer, had died. He was around the age I am now (28). Apparently living life was just too much for him. A few months after the funeral, which I didn't attend, I ran into our Seminole friend at a gas station. He was wearing eye shadow and had a pink streak in his hair. He said: *I always knew it would happen. He was miserable.* He was clearly sad. They had all been really close friends growing up: the newly deceased, my brother, and this gothic Native American fellow. Instead of a eulogy, they played that Pixies song that's at the end of *Fight Club*, you know, when Edward Norton and Helena Bonham Carter hold hands and watch as the world literally crumbles around them.

BUDD DWYER

I watched *Faces of Death* exactly one time with my friends when we were teenagers. There were a lot of overblown, laughable, fake-out deaths, and then there were the others, the truly disturbing and horrific ones, the ones that come home with you, leave a bad taste in your mouth. The public suicide of Budd Dwyer is the one that stuck with me. At the time, I didn't know who he was, or why he did what he did—I just knew that this one was real, a man blowing his brains out on camera, and that I was sick with that knowledge, the fact that I wanted to look. Turns out he was a Pennsylvanian politician who had been accused of taking a bribe. He set up a press conference. After the cameras started rolling, he started in on this speech, declaring his innocence for about four minutes, and then he took this big-ass handgun from a manila envelope and said, *Don't, don't. Look, look this will hurt someone.* He put the gun into his mouth and blew the top of his skull off. I took the image home with me and slept on it. It invaded my dreams for a few weeks, and then, just as quickly as it came, it left me. Could it be that my brain couldn't handle it? Was it repressed? Who knows? Anyway, I hadn't thought about Budd for years until a few weeks back. I was in my car, that Filter song "Hey Man, Nice Shot" came on, and I saw Budd shoving that gun into his mouth all over again. It was the first time in my life that I felt like he must have had his reasons. If we had only questioned the image, interrogated our bias and opted out of the popular notion that he was just an insane man who was at his breaking point, we would have discovered the truth, whatever the truth might have been. Instead, we sensationalized what, when looked at in a different light, could arguably be considered the last public execution in American history—and then we watched it on a loop.

HIV

My brother's out of prison and staying at our parent's. I'm living there too, when I'm not out partying, gone for days on end. I come home one day and go upstairs to shave before going out for the night, my ride parked out front and waiting. I hum some stupid song, ignoring my dad on my way up to my bedroom. On my way out, my dad calls me in to talk with him for a minute. He's engulfed in a cloud of cigarette smoke when I get downstairs, watching the news. He tells me to have a seat. I sit down. Then he says, *Your brother's old roommate called.* And I'm like, *Yeah, so what? What's it have to do with me?* And then it starts. He tells me about how this roommate of my brother's said that one of the guys my brother used to share needles with had recently been diagnosed with HIV. We'd been sharing razors since he'd been back, out on parole, and, being the clumsy fucks we were born to be, we always ended up with blood on our faces—to this day I massacre my face when I shave. My dad says, *Your mom took him to get tested.* He says, *Don't share razors or anything until after we know a little more about what is going on,* and all I can think is, *Too late,* but I don't tell him that. Instead of staying at home to brood, I leave to go out for the night, a scalding clump of fear in my chest like a cannon ball, and keep thinking, *My brother has just sentenced me to death. He has finally done it. He is killing me.* Two days later, I make another trek home and my parents tell me not to worry about it, he tested negative. *Your brother is going to be okay.* My relief is astounding, like, I can't even explain it. I guess it was a thing like quasars or black holes or the universe expanding—incredible, nearly extraterrestrial, something you can hardly scratch the surface of before being forced to confront just how small and inconsequential your entire existence is and has been and will always be. And in the midst of all of this, I've been having revelations about my future. I'm in love with a good friend of mine, maybe the best I've ever known, and what a feeling it is to love someone more than you've ever loved yourself, or anybody else for that matter— something I find difficult even now to describe. If I were infected, I wouldn't date. It would be unfair. But now, now that I know for certain that I'm not infected, the gumption to spill the ooze is bubbling. It's scalding. Maybe my new love and I will build something beyond us. I want to live with her in the middle of the forest, in a tiny castle made of wood.

FRESHMAN

Freshman year of high school I'm in a band. They are new friends with mutual interests. Knowing how to play music is secondary to everything. Being in a band, that's what matters. We play crappy covers of nu metal songs, sometimes grunge. We suck, but who cares? We alternate between each other's houses for practice. We don't even have a drummer. The first time they ever come over to my house, my brother tells us to come into the basement and hang with him for a while before we start. When we get down there he has all this cocaine cut up and in lines on the end table. He asks if we want any. I say no right away, and then look at my friends, hoping their responses echo mine. They look nervous as fuck. I get it; they're trying to play it cool. I tell my brother, *Fuck that, we aren't doing that shit*, but he's determined to get somebody in on it, either because he's the loneliest person I've ever known, or because, if he has some company, maybe he'll feel less guilty about doing it by himself. *Oh, c'mon. It isn't that bad. It hardly even does anything*, he says. I leave the basement, calling for my friends to take my lead. But they stay behind, feigning small talk, as I walk up the stairs and into the kitchen. Not five minutes later, they emerge, all jittery, with young hearts about to pump out through their chests and onto the floor. This is the first impression, the thing that stamped our friendship into the battered thing it was destined to become.

ACID PHONE

My brother wanted me to do acid with him, but I was only thirteen, and I was too scared, so I told him I didn't want to do it, and he shook his head and said, *Fuck you, then.* He liked to mess with me, so he told me if I was going to be a pussy about it and not do it with him, be careful about what I touched or ate or drank for the next few days. *Liquid acid*, he said. *I can put it on anything and you'd never know it was there. Next you know, the carpet's licking at your feet and the walls are dripping sweat into your eyes.* For some reason, an irrational fear, I was convinced that he'd smeared it on the telephone receiver. This was back in the time of landlines, and it was the only phone in the house. I'd have to touch it sooner or later, I knew that, but I already felt like a crazy person and I couldn't afford to be any crazier than I already was. It was all a grandiose setup, a trick. I left the phone alone for nearly a week. I was trying to preserve my sanity.

BREAKING, ENTERING, SMOKING

The first time I inhaled I was thirteen or fourteen. I'd smoked cigarettes before, but I'd been faking it, I'd never inhaled. It burned like hell, that first time. I hated the way it felt, the smell, the burn, I hated all of it. But I kept doing it anyway. I had something to prove. We chain-smoked a whole pack, me and two of my friends, late one night after spending a few hours out and about in various neighborhoods, breaking into cars. That's how we got them, the cigarettes and the lighter. We'd been getting into unlocked cars for a few months already, because that's what the boredom of this town bred, but one time we actually came away from it with something more than just our shame. We got forty dollars, a Walkman, some shitty CDs, and three packs of cigarettes—all from one car. Afterward, we lay out on my friend's trampoline in his backyard. It was a summer night, clear, and we admired our loot in the moonlight, filling our lungs with smoke and talking about all the girls at school we couldn't stop thinking about, how we'd love to sweat into their palms, feel our saliva swath across their tongues, and, if we played our cards right, tremble inside them in the comfort of their homes while their parents worked nights to put food in their stomachs and meat on their bones.

TENNIS BALLS

My dad had this friend he hadn't seen in like twenty years. Supposedly he was a great jazz musician who just couldn't seem to get his shit together. He drank. Too much, they said. And he lost everything because of it, became a homeless untouchable who walked the streets by day and slept under our city's bridges by night. My dad saw him on the street one day, recognized him beneath his raggedy-ass street clothes, and brought him home, set him up with a cot in the basement, helped him dry out, and then told him to get back out into the city and find himself a job. Sometimes my mom would give him rides. I'd go with them. We'd take him downtown, or sometimes farther east, and just drop him off. My mom would ask him what time she should pick him up and he'd tell her, *No, I'll walk back. Truly it's okay. You have done more than enough.* And, remarkably, he would always make it back by dinner, no matter how far it was we'd left him. I remember that he spent Christmas with us. He gave me an old tennis ball as a gift. I think it was even wrapped.

It was brown from use, worn nearly smooth. It was a little strange to be honest. But he had nothing, absolutely nothing, except for some raggedy clothes and a guitar he considered his soul. And truth is, I came to really love my tennis ball. It was the gesture, really. I don't recall him giving anything to anybody else, and, at the time, I thought that meant something. A week or two later, my parents kicked him out. He'd been drinking the Listerine to get a good buzz going, both in the mornings and in the evenings. Once night my mom said to my dad: *What's going on? I've bought two bottles of Listerine in a week.* My dad's heart had sunk into him. I could see it on his slack face. He knew what was what, he always does.

I kept the tennis ball for a long time. One day our dog took off with it and dropped it in the middle of the road. I went after it but wasn't quick enough. It rolled through a garden-hose puddle—then the last thing I remember was the sound it made: *thud-thud thud-thudding* in the guts of the gutter.

Picture this: Budd Dwyer at his last press conference—cameras rolling, flashbulbs flashing, ratings rising, watchers watching, recorders recording, watchers watching, rewinders rewinding, watchers watching, pausers pausing, watchers watching, pausers pausing, watchers watch—

REDNECK NEIGHBOR PT. 1

Growing up, our neighbor across the way was an alcoholic in his late thirties or early forties who lived with his mom. He was a hillbilly from Texas. He walked the walk and talked the talk—loved all things beer and automobiles, all things pussy and g-string. He told me once that he wanted "Freebird" played at his wedding, if he ever met a girl worthy of marriage, and then, another time, he said he wanted the same song played at his funeral. And I thought: *What's the difference?* His hair looked like burnt wool. He also had a face full of beard. He liked to think he was good friends with my parents and came over often to visit damn near daily. You could tell when he visited with them he was trying his best to behave himself. When they weren't around, he'd say the filthiest things—like, if he saw a nice-looking woman out with her kids or walking the dog, he would pause, mid-sentence, stare her down, and say something like: *Goddamn, Jimmy Dean! Look at that. I'd eat the peanuts out of her shit.* He also had this odd crush on my sister. You could tell. It was in the way he looked at her, the words he used when speaking to her. And even though he was obnoxious, she was gentle with him in her gestures and attitude, though she didn't have to be, and all this even after all the ugliness had come out of him. See, he had come over drunk one night after my sister had left the house, because he was jealous of her new boyfriend. He made the mistake of telling my dad exactly how he felt about it. He said, *She's a slut for getting with that nigger.* And my dad, the look in his eyes, I thought he was going to kill him. He got up from the table and right into our neighbor's face with his face and said he would kill him if he ever spoke that way about his daughter again. Our neighbor, poor man, collapsed beneath the weight of his tears, begging my dad's forgiveness, and my dad, he sat him down and said, *I can't forgive you, no, not for that, but I'll give you a cup of coffee.* And so it was—for the next two hours: the two of them sucking back smoke, drinking coffee, trying to cleanse themselves of the demons of their pasts through a shared knowledge of trauma. But then my dad, he got all serious like he does, and said, *You can't blame anybody but yourself for your problems. You are your problems.* At first I thought he said it for the benefit of our neighbor. But then I thought about it. I mean, it was different than the usual preachments I was used to. There was a rare quaver in his voice, a choked-up sound. He said it just so he could say it to himself, because he realized that in a way, he was being confronted with a mirror, and he suddenly felt terrified for himself and everybody he'd ever loved.

ANOTHER
DEAD

The first time I met this guy it was at a DIY show at this old auto repair shop some of my friends rented. I was there so often I was nearly a fixture. We were drinking whiskey, me and my buddy who played in one of the bands. There were a lot people there. We were partying on the roof after the show, watching fireworks illuminate the downtown skyline. I went inside to piss and when I came out there was this guy with a ripped shirt, a nose-piercing, and long unwashed hair. I was walking past him to get back outside when he grabbed me by the shirt, pulled me in close, and said, *You're a computer, man. We're all computers.* I laughed, and tried to shake him off me, but he gripped me tighter and said: *CPU. CPU. CPU.* And then I just lost it. I shoved him with all my weight into the refrigerator and walked back out onto the rooftop. When the door closed I said, *Refrigerator.* Turns out, dude was a heroin user, though

I'm sure he was on something else that first run-in we had at the show. He started selling to people in the music scene. I didn't like it at all. But there were so many of my friends who were friends with him that I had to be cordial when we bumped into each other. I didn't see him for a long time, and then, maybe a year later, I heard from somebody that he was in college and off the drugs. And I thought, Okay, good. Even then I didn't really like him I thought it was cool he was figuring things out. And then, out of nowhere, he died. He was my age when he died, plus or minus a few months. What happened was he relapsed, one time, overdosed, and died. And I felt sadder than sad. And then I felt guilty for feeling sad. Honestly, I didn't understand what it was I was feeling and it went on like that for a while. Then, one day I realized I wasn't sad at all, probably never had been. I almost broke down when I thought of it. I was driving and I held in the tears so I wouldn't crash the car. When you realize something like that, that you don't feel a great loss or even sadness for someone who has recently passed away, it comes out of nowhere, hits you in the teeth like a ton of bricks. It is the saddest kind of sad—the saddest sad of all.

PRIMO

You ever smoke coke-dusted weed? Shit, the guy didn't even tell me what it was until after we'd smoked it. Luckily it didn't freak me out like I thought it would. It was just like there were these tiny angels climbing up and down a million microscopic structures crosshatched in my veins. I couldn't stop smiling. My heart was trying out for the Olympics. I could just die, right then, and be happy about the next day's obituary because I had felt *that* good at least once while I was alive and that was enough and it felt worth it. I was like fourteen or fifteen. It seems like everything happened when I was fourteen or fifteen. But maybe that's the way it is with everybody.

REDNECK NEIGHBOR PT. 2

When I was into skateboarding and punk music, our neighbor helped me build a quarter-pipe out of wood we stole from various construction sites around some new housing developments in the area. It was about four or five feet high and the same in width. It took a few days to build it. It was hot, the summer sun scorching through civilities, making people cranky and fiendish for a breeze. When we finished tapping the last nail into place, we stepped back and admired it. He felt proud of his handiwork and tried running up it in his cowboy boots. On his way up he slipped, but he caught himself on the coping with his ribcage, cussing like mad into the heat. Thing is, he didn't spill a drop of his beer, and there was the cigarette, still clenched between his lips and smoking up into his eyes, so now he had something else to be proud of. *See that,* he said, *didn't spill one fucking drop*. He had two broken ribs. For the next several weeks he taped his chest up at night, drank during the day to keep the pain away. Shit, he did that anyway, the drinking, but the tape—the tape was something to get used to.

RECENT
BEDROOM

I couldn't fall asleep because my brother and his girlfriend were fucking in the other room. She was really loud, sounded like she was being murdered and liked it. I put the pillow over my head. I could still hear her though. She was something. It got my dick hard hearing her like that. She was a good-looking girl. It made me feel guilty getting boners directly linked to her voice, her image, her body under my brother's pumping, but I couldn't figure a way to get it out of my head. They were just rubbing it in, night after night. I was surprised my parents couldn't hear it, but they were downstairs and the way that house was set up, noises seemed to keep to their own levels.

One day, while my brother was in prison for theft, I went to the mall with his girlfriend. Afterwards, we found ourselves in his bedroom when my parents weren't home. She had just bought him some clothes for when he got out of prison and she wanted me to try them on, model them a bit. So I did. I modeled the shit out of those clothes. And that's when it happened. She grabbed the waist band of my jeans and pulled me close, unzipping. She grabbed my dick, which at that point was harder than marble. I let her touch it a minute, and then, even though I'd been dreaming about this for nearly a year, I pushed her back onto the bed and zipped my pants up. *I think you should leave,* I said. *Please,* I said, blushing, *would you please leave.* And she wasn't even upset. She understood what was what and left without a word. I wanted to cry, but I didn't. I kept it inside of me. Who was she kidding, anyway? She never wanted me—never, not once. She missed my brother. She wanted to feel our shared blood throb into her through the motions of my body—and I blew it. After she left, I couldn't stop thinking about what it would have been like. I could've shown her something, something she probably should've known. I could have shown her just how hard it is for a person to fit inside my brother's skin. It's a dangerous game. I didn't want to risk anything.

MISMATCHED
SOCKS

I don't recall having ever worn a matching pair of socks.

DEPRESSION

My dad would go through bouts of depression so bad some days I wouldn't want to leave him alone. It was at its worst when my mom wasn't home. He would hang his head, silently, and mope about the house. He would cry easily about the littlest things he viewed on the television. Sometimes he would leave the house when he got like that and I'd worry that he'd never make it back home. I worried he'd leave us for another family in another city, in another state. But mostly I worried that he would just flat out get up and leave us for another world. I'm not alone in this thinking, either. My sister had the same thoughts, and I'm sure others in the family did, too. Sometimes he'd talk about life like it wasn't worth living. Most of the time, I believed him. He'd take off in the mornings to go drink coffee with his friends, and I'd think, *This is it. He's going to drive off a bridge or overpass. He's going to noose up in a gas station bathroom or take a blade to his wrists in the parking lot at Braum's.*

NAMES OF BANDS I WANT TO START

Burt Cobain

Crotch Rockets from the Crypt

Attaché Death Mask

James Weave and the Pumpkin Splatters

Joy Addition

The Fairies

Out of the Blue Balls, Into the Black Sacks

The Liver Spots

Las Haggis

Sombrero Ninja Hotplate

Shitty Kitten

Twisters and Twizzlers

The Refried Bean Conspiracy

The Twelfth-floor Escalators

Troy Division

PHONE SEX

My brother used to use my dad's credit card to call places like 1-800-BIG-TITS so that he could jerk off to faceless fat chicks and their heavy-handed breathing techniques. The phone and credit card bills would come in the mail. They would be in the hundreds, sometimes thousands of dollars. I've seen my dad beat the crap out of my brother for doing shit like this. I won't lie, it happened sometimes. It was hard for me to feel bad for my brother or my dad. They couldn't control themselves. My brother had to listen to women breathe into the phone to achieve orgasm and my dad had to beat him to feel like he had a handle on the situation. I usually hid in my room, turned up some music to drown out the noise. It started happening more frequently—the phone calls, the punishments, the in-my-room-all-alone-with-the-music-up hour—and then, one day, my mom and dad instigated a new rule. There would only be one phone allowed in the house and when they went to bed at night they would unplug it and hide it in their bedroom. What kind of shit is that? *This sucks*, I thought. Just because my older brother couldn't stop playing with his dick, I had to suffer for it. Imagine that. I used to spend endless hours on the phone—now, not so much. And there was another problem, too. I always worried about the receiver. *Why does it feel so greasy? Is that a pubic hair between the 2 and the 3 on the dial pad? Can I catch something? Where's the Vaseline?*

POOP BOOTS

My brother and sister got along for the most part. But they also had a crazy streak. I remember one night. Summer most likely. Full moon, possibly, I mean it would make sense. My sister and her best friend are hanging out upstairs. There's either some early-nineties rap or some pseudo-hippy shit on the stereo. Anyway, it is a night like all the others—my dad at the dining room table chain-smoking, my mom reading in her bedroom, me on the couch watching Dracula. Things are normal. There is this quietness to the air. My brother isn't home. I am petting the dog, admiring the tumor on his back, when it happens: a scream like someone had just been stabbed with an electric turkey carver pulses through the wood and sheetrock and pipes of the house. I perk up and look at my dad. My dad looks at the ceiling, looks back at me. His look is a look of worry, but he still doesn't get up from his chair. I think: *That's strange, Bela Legosi isn't biting anyone at the moment*, and then I hear water rushing through the pipes. The faucet to the upstairs bathtub—laughter mixed in with the wetness drifts through the sheetrock. Sometimes I wonder if my sister isn't a lesbian. She and her friends hold hands. They seem so close. Now I imagine them taking a shower together. You can hear them. They're both in there. What about the scream though—the laughter? Suddenly the water stops, the laughter stops, heavy feet quick across the floor come rushing down the stairs like a fall, and my sister and her best friend present themselves before us, ready to explain it all. And out it comes, no filter. The story goes something like this. My sister's friend wanted to try on my sister's Doc Martens. My sister said: *Sure. Try them on.* And she did, she tried them on—well, kind of. See, here's the problem. When she got her sockless foot into the first boot, a room-temperature, dog-food-like mush slowly oozed between her toes. *Gag, gag, gag, gag, gag.* She pulled the boot off immediately. The smell of it, I can only imagine. It was shit all right. But it wasn't from a dog or cat. *This is human*, she said. *Human shit.* My dad laughs. *How can you tell?* And she says: *I can just tell, man. It's human. I'm telling you. It's human.* And it is human. It's his own son's shit, my brother's shit. When my brother catches wind of what happened he's oh-so-proud of himself, like he thinks he's done something good with his life with this stunt. He could make a living at it, maybe, if he applied himself. *She deserved it*, he says. And see, that's it, he'd given my sister some money to get him some weed or something and she spent it all or smoked it all—it still remains a mystery—but he never got his money back or his weed or whatever it was, but shit in her boot, that'll make it even. I think it is a well-played prank, but I am young and stupid and don't know shit. And that isn't the end of it, either. My sister and her friend wipe the pee off their vaginas with his pillow case the following weekend, and my brother, he doesn't suspect a thing. There are a lot of things that happen in this world—bad things, strange things, gross and despicable things—but this one, the piss on the pillow, every time I think of it, it makes me smile.

NAZIS

My parents took me to the Renaissance Festival when I was ten. It was my first one. I'd heard good things from kids in my class. They were right. Everything intrigued me—the knights, the wenches, the guy locked in the stockade, being punished for a misdeed, and even all the weird hippies selling incense and soaps at their makeshift booths. But what really stuck with me, what put a cramp in my side, were the skinheads. At that point in my life, I didn't know what these people were all about. All I knew is they didn't have anything to do with the Renaissance Festival—no, they were more WWII than anything. I'd seen those symbols on the History Channel. When we walked past them, I could feel the sickly power of all those twisted crosses in the manic pacing of my heart beat, and I wondered about the words in the pamphlets they were passing out, and whether or not the tattoos covering their arms and necks and legs had been worth the pain. A pit formed in my stomach, a metallic taste in my mouth, but I didn't really feel bad—just different, strange, slightly molested by their presence. They looked mean as fuck, like they would just crackle your teeth for smiling, or knock you over into the mud—then beat the shit out of you for being a "nigger." They were handing out pamphlets filled with hate speech, I'm sure, recruitment ads. There were like twenty to thirty of them, men and women and children. I couldn't stop thinking about them. They were ruining my day. The fear was palpable—you could snatch it from the air. Why? I'm blonde, have hazel eyes and white skin. My dad told me to pay no mind. *They're just a bunch of ignorant, misguided kids who probably never had anybody around to care for them when they were growing up.* It was true, sometimes my dad spits it just right, so that I can go on and feel all right about the world he gave me. Then again, I'd heard him say racial slurs more than once in my life, so who exactly was he in this big, complex picture? Just because you keep it hidden doesn't mean it isn't right there inside you—a vast stain on your heart.

COWBOYS AND INDIANS

I wanted to be a cowboy and an Indian—I wanted to be anything with a weapon that went *bang* or *fffwap* or *kaboom* in my hands. I wanted to shoot a missile through the space between the hot June sky and the sinking sun. I'd sing cowboy songs to the dense air, dreaming of astronauts, wondering what time I'd wake up in the morning to go fishing with my friends. I wanted more than anything to feel connected to history, to feel connected to the world. I wondered about the buffalos that roamed these plains before they became cities. I envisioned carcasses for miles and miles, burning skinless in the sun forever, maggots asleep in the tragedy of their wounds. I wondered if someday some non-human would wonder about the people who had lived in these cities, way back in the day, before they became ruin-strewn tourist attractions replete with landing pads for alien spaceships.

DISNEY VACATION

Another summer, or maybe the same summer, I'm eleven and hanging out with my brother and this kid we go to church with. We are at the neighborhood park, swinging, shooting hoops, dicking around on the seesaw, and then, out of nowhere, my brother has this little baggy out of his pocket and he's asking this kid we go to church with if he wants any. The bag is filled with these tiny yellowish crystals. The kid says: *What is it?* And my brother, he must sense some amount of uncoolness in the kid, because he just shrugs, says: *Oh, nothing, just some candy,* and puts the baggy back into his pocket. We shoot hoops for a while. Then my brother stops and points his finger at my best friend's house. He says: *You want to go into that house with us?* The kid is hesitant to answer. His face is like *what?* and his hands and feet are nervous. *What?* My brother shrugs. *It's no biggie, they're friends. They just happen to be out of town this weekend.* But the kid makes this silly hand motion and says: *Oh, no, no, I can't do that. Actually, I'm late. I've got to go* and he leaves, just like that, and me and my brother, we go home, not saying another thing about it.

Later that night, my brother wakes me. He says: *We're doing it?* And I say: *What the—what?* And he says: *We're going into the house. Come on, get dressed.* I hesitate, but only for a minute.

When we get there, we spend a few minutes figuring out the best form of entry. We check the doors but they're all locked. All the windows are locked, too, except for the storm window, which my brother pushes in with his fist. He snakes down into the dark without a word. Objects crash around him—pictures, trophies, trinkets, and I whisper down: *You okay?* And he says: *Yeah, I'm fine. Come on, I'll let you in through the back door.*

The sliding glass door at the back of the house opens. I'm inside. We start in the kitchen, snooping through the cupboards. Find a bottle of vodka tucked behind some crackers. My brother fills a glass, no mixer, and drinks down about a third of it, and then asks if I want any, but I shake my head, *nah.* We make our way up the stairs, looking through all of their stuff along the way. Exhilarated, my heart races faster and faster, but I feel dirty, too, so much muck of confusion making its slow drive into me.

My best friend's parent's bedroom is a goldmine we're not expecting. While looking through the dresser drawer we come across a Penthouse. Claudia Schiffer's in it, showing her stuff—tits, legs, ass, all of it out and on display. I try to play off my excitement but can feel the heat in my face, the blood rushing. In another drawer, a video cassette in oversized packaging (a porno), and a couple of rubber penises—my brother calls them *dildos*. I pull them out and look them over. One of them is about ten inches long. At the base there's a place to put the batteries. I turn them over in my hands, imagining my best friend's mother putting them inside her. I feel slightly sick, slightly turned on, slightly embarrassed. Suddenly, I want to leave. I feel wrong being there. My brother has the porno going on the large screen TV, watching with vague interest while drinking his liquor. I say, *Hey, I want to go. I'm getting tired.* And he says, *Okay, we'll go, just give me a minute,* and he closes the door.

I go into my best friend's bedroom and lay down on his bed. I close my eyes. I wait. I start counting sheep to alleviate the boredom—not really sheep, just aloud to myself in the dark. I open my eyes, I close them, I open them, and I wait. I count. I wonder what could possibly be taking so long. I count some more. I think about Claudia Schiffer's perfect boobs, stop thinking about them, start again, stop again, decide to lay on my stomach so I don't start jacking off on instinct in my best friend's bed. Laying on your boner isn't exactly comfortable. I'm starting to think we'll get into trouble—that someone will find out what we've done, that maybe we will end up in a jail for kids somewhere off in the sticks. I'm grinding my teeth, eyes closed, face down, reaching for a thought that will make me feel just the slightest bit cleaner inside, when I hear my brother walking through the hallway, calling my name, signaling departure. And to this day, when someone says my name, I feel this unnamable force surround me. It comes on at the back of my neck, then full on, cold and familiar, and tugs at me, trying to pull me away from one place and set me down in another.

TRAPPING

I never meant to hurt anybody. I just wanted to snag me an Apache. I was ten. We were just playing, that's all—games don't hurt anybody. We were playing cowboys and Indians. When you want to trick the enemy, you have to outsmart them, be one step ahead. My brother and I were at the treehouse we'd built, on the outskirts of our neighborhood, shooting sticks into the trees. We were the only ones that ever went there, aside from a straggler or two every once in a blue moon.

That day I chose to be a cowboy. We fought invisible Apaches in the woods. We ran all over the place, panting and sweating, shooting down our foes. But even when you're young, you eventually tire of the hunt. We rested against a tree trunk, catching our breath, devising a plan. Then we did it. Right before we left, we nailed three seven-inch nails through a two-by-four and hid it under some leaves. Right above that, there was a branch. We figured rope would be something the Indians would find useful, so we tied a piece of rope from this branch right above the nails, but it was just out of reach. So if an Apache wanted it, he would have to jump to grab it—three upturned nails awaiting his foot on landing. We didn't think anything of it. It was just a game. But it didn't even take two whole days before somebody actually got hurt. It was my brother's friend's older sister. She was probably out there smoking pot with some friends. Apparently she wanted the rope. Maybe it annoyed her seeing it hang there like that. All three nails entered the bottom or her foot and came out the top when she landed, rope in hand. Probably hurt like hell. I hope the rope was worth it. I felt really terrible when I found out about it. But nobody suspected a thing, so I kept my mouth shut. Even now, all these years later, I wish I could say something. Maybe I'm saying it now. In the off chance you're still out there, please forgive me. I never meant to hurt anybody.

BREAKING BONES

This girl who was my brother's age, I was best friends with her little brother, so I was over at their house quite a lot—swimming, playing video games, watching TV, or, more often than not, waiting for some kind of drama to unfold. They had a pool in their backyard. I liked looking at his sister when she donned a bathing suit in the summers. But it was winter and school was back in session. She didn't like school. I was over one day, my bare feet comfy and padded atop sea foam green carpet. I thought she was an oracle of some kind because she was always messing with Ouija boards and crystals. She wore darker eyeliner than most girls, smudges of it, and listened to Marilyn Manson and Ministry. She had a baggy black shirt on, which swallowed her form. When we heard what she was planning to do to herself to get out of going to school, my friend and I and their brother, the middle child, gathered around her and watched. She took a normal claw hammer from her purse. Then she lit some incense, biding time. After a minute or two she pressed her palm flat to the floor, making an angle of her arm, and started pounding on her forearm with the hammer. She was getting it pretty good, too. *Thud, thud, thud.* She had candles burning. Vanilla. We watched her with interest and admiration, but deep down we felt sick too, it was written on our faces. *This girl needs help*, I thought. *This is so messed up.* Just when I thought I couldn't watch anymore, she gave up. She couldn't break it, not even close, her bones were too strong. And it was all for nothing because her parents made her go to school anyway, with eight inches of purples and blues up and down her left arm, and thick globs of mascara making her eyes look as though they'd been left out in the sun too long.

JUMPING FROM A BRIDGE

I jumped off a bridge once. The girl I'd loved for the last two years was there. We were hanging out around Cow Skin Creek, smoking cigarettes, skipping stones over the water, talking shit on the influx of jocks at the middle school. I jumped into the water on a whim, treaded heavily with shoes and jeans on, and hoped she would fall in love with me for doing so. But her eyes, they just looked the same, dull and dead inside.

Maybe that's why I loved her so much. I felt the same way. Empty.

When we were walking back up over the bridge to go home for dinner, that's when I did it. I jumped up onto the rail without a thought, and did a front flip, letting my body fall twenty feet. I over-rotated though. Water feels like cement when you're coming at it from that kind of height, at that kind of velocity. Knocked the wind clean out of my chest, and my face felt all puffy with blood, and my nose, water shot up it like you wouldn't believe, felt like it was sloshing around inside my brain. But even still, approaching her back on top of the bridge, all I could do was smile. I wanted her to love me like I loved her, which was foolishly, selfishly, unhealthily. I wanted to consume her, and wanted to be consumed by her. Even though we believed we felt things more deeply than most, we were both consumed by our mutual distrust of emotions. We didn't know shit, but we felt everything, even the static sound of the wind vibrating through our bones. It was too intense to feel. We hated it. And so we shielded ourselves with masks. She did her drugs and I drank. And when we got used to being numb, hiding behind our layers, the desire to feel again became a hunger. So she started searching for love in backseats in random cars and sloppy beds, and I burned myself with cigarettes and smoldering incense sticks, telling myself that love feels exactly the same as pain, only slightly better, only slightly more real.

COUGH SYRUP

My dad used to drink cough syrup like it was going out of style. He was doing that shit way before Lil Wayne even materialized as a sperm. He'd sit at the table and drink half a bottle straight down and smoke cigarettes in a daze. One night he got so looped he was out of his mind. He kept telling my sister to massage his brain. *Please,* he'd say. *Massage my brain. Massage my medulla oblongata.* And so she went along with it. She started rubbing her hands through his hair vigorously, giggling. And then he started saying shit like: *You are massaging my brain. You are massaging my medulla oblongata,* in this weird, loud, trembling vibrato. This went on for like two hours. It was better than watching a movie. I sat on the couch, and watched, laughing until I could no longer breathe. My lungs hurt so bad I thought I'd spit blood. Then he told her to stop. So she stopped for a minute, and he looked up at her from his chair and said: *I need to sit down. My ass needs to sit down.*

She laughed. *Dad, you are already sitting. Don't lie to me*, he said. *Get me a chair. I need to sit my ass down.*

THE SIGN OF SATAN

When I was in second grade I drew a pentagram on the chalkboard during indoor recess and told my friend to check it out. *What is it?* he said. And I said, *I don't know, but if you turn it upside down, it's the sign of the devil—at least that's what my brother told me.* The next day an angry parent showed up to confront me, and I got pulled out into the hall to explain myself. My teacher said: *Troy, Troy, Troy… Where on earth did you learn about this stuff?* I started crying. *It was a joke,* I told them. *I don't know what the sign of Satan looks like. I just made it up.* I thought I could get away with it. But I didn't. They took me back into the classroom and made me draw the symbol for them. I did. I should have made something up. I always had a problem with telling the truth. I always told the truth, even if a lie could get me out of trouble, which was not very bright on my end of things. *Well,* my teacher told me, *for making up a symbol you did a pretty accurate job.* I didn't get in any trouble, but I was never allowed to hang out with my friend again. And a few months later, he started calling me names and shaming other kids into not liking me. He told people that I worshiped the devil, did human sacrifices, and drank goat's blood. I didn't worship the devil. I didn't worship anything. I just wanted to be a kid who wasn't alone in the world. But that day I learned an important lesson. Sharing: it's the fastest assurer for your future loneliness.

DEATH IS A TRACTOR

Impermanence is a fact. Nothing lasts forever exactly as it is. Take my great-uncle. He's ninety-four years old. He's in great shape, he just keeps going. But recently he fell ill with pneumonia and was hospitalized for a couple weeks, and my mother flew into Wichita thinking this would be the final goodbye. It wasn't, but still, things change, always. Nothing is ever the same. We all know it's only a matter of time, for all of us, and everything—and I mean *everything*. Doesn't mean time stops. In fact, that's the issue. I always hear people complaining about death. *I don't want to die, I just couldn't handle it.* Thing is, though, you can't experience your own death, you can only imagine it, and in my mind, that is the greatest fiction of all. Death is a fiction you edit and rewrite a million times in your mind, something you take home and sleep on— and then one day it happens to you, the manuscript is finished. But the beauty is, when it happens you won't even know the difference. When my great-uncle dies, which will hopefully be in the distant future, I will always remember the time he let me ride on the tractor with him when I was seven years old. He was drinking a Coors, the breeze was cool, and we were one and alive in a world that is relentlessly spinning, a world whose memory can only be written. Like that, for instance—the tractor, the illness, the eventual death—and just knowing that it's all a lie.

COLLAPSIBLE
LUNGS

Christmas day, the annual call to my parents in Arizona, and it doesn't feel the same. It isn't joyful. There's dread in their voices. And soon enough I find out, the dread I'm hearing is the dread of held secrets, a secret they know isn't timed right but must come out because they know I would want it that way.

We start off with pleasantries. *Merry Christmas, I miss you*, and, *What are your plans for dinner this evening? Have anything special planned?* This goes on as long as you'd expect and then it staggers beyond. My dad asks about the weather. I tell him it's cold, as it always is in Kansas in December. Finally there is silence—tension thick as gristle and bone—and then, finally, they come out with it.

Your brother's in the hospital.

My chest feels like it's been battered with a jackhammer. I can't get any air into my lungs. By the time I catch my breath, I hear myself saying the words *what happened* even though I already know the answer.

He was out in the yard. Three guys jumped him. Beat him nearly to death.

Is he okay?

He'll live, but one of his lungs collapsed and his face is so bad you wouldn't even recognize him.

Just got in with the wrong crowd, is all.

How do you get in with the right crowd, when you're in prison?

This is true.

Jeez.

We're sorry to drop this on you on Christmas but we thought you'd like to know, you know. You get mad at us when we don't tell you things. Anyway, don't let it ruin your day. We love you. Can't wait to see you next time we're in town.

Love you. Bye.

I hang up the phone. All I can do is think about my brother spending Christmas in the hospital, all hooked up to machines, hoses and wires coming out of him, helping him breathe, monitoring his heart, all alone. I feel like crying, but usually don't cry when it comes to him, so instead of being a normal human being, I sit in front of the computer and type out a small series of words.

I

Love

You,

You

Fucker

And right then, my eyelids well. I close my eyes, open them, see the words on the computer screen, glowing there, and wait the necessary amount of time to feel assured that they are etched onto my heart and had always been there. Then I left-click and hold on the mouse, scrolling upward over the words, making the background blue instead of white, doing over and over again until I feel sufficiently filled, like I don't need to look at the words to make it any more real than it already is. I reach my pinky a full inch up and to the left and firmly press DELETE. The screen goes white. *What's next?*

This is the only way I know how to love.

GIRLFRIEND JR.

A few months back I was visiting a website of obituaries for the Wichita area because my uncle had recently passed and I needed something to concrete the reality for me, to help get me past an uncertain stage of mourning. But I got a lot more than I bargained for. In fact, I didn't even make it to his obituary until a few days later, because I discovered the name of one of my adolescent love interest's husband among the names of the recently departed. It really hit me. He was my age. He couldn't have died of natural causes. Of course, he could have, but upon further reading it was quite clear that it was anything but natural—or maybe more natural than I'd like to admit. He'd served a tour or two or three in Afghanistan or Iraq, or both, and apparently, once he was back and safe at home, he still heard the screams and the bombs—saw the tracers zooming past his ears while watching TV at night. I stopped reading when I felt the smooth rounded edges of my heart become hard angles. I got onto Facebook and looked up my dear friend from the past. They had a child together. I skimmed through her photo albums—I'm going to ballpark the age of their son at around five years old. I found out that they had actually been separated or divorced for about a year, maybe it was someone who had told me that, or maybe I gathered it from the pictures and newsfeeds as I traced them back through time. Anyway, I don't know why people do the things they do, but however horrific, selfish, and tragic they may be, nobody has any kind of right to judge them, because they know depths you have never even come close to feeling. *You're still alive, aren't you?*

Or are you?

CAR CRASH

One day, when I was about nine, my best friend and I were playing catch at the park when we heard a loud crash. We threw out mitts to the ground, let the ball roll through the grass, and ran the two blocks up to the main road. We were the first ones to arrive, and what we saw was too horrible for our young minds to fathom. An SUV had t-boned a little sedan, and the driver of the little car had been pushed all the way into the back seat. We circled around the wreckage, too afraid to do anything. The people in the SUV were fine, but, like us, they were too afraid of what they'd find in the other car to do anything either, so they just sat curbside with tears in their eyes. Finally, a lady came out of her house and said an ambulance was on its way. We approached the car, keeping a little distance, eyes wide, searching. The driver of the sedan looked really bad, completely unconscious, and I wondered what it even meant to die. Then the ambulance and firemen arrived. The police arrived too. They started cutting at the car to get the driver out. I got a better look and saw the driver was a teenager, just a few years older than me. The way he was positioned in the back seat, you could see his head arched back, facing up. He hadn't moved once during the five minutes we'd been there. Then he retched. Blood shot from his lips, smacking against the headliner, and dripped back down onto his face. *Drip drip, drip drip, drip drip.* They finally got him out and onto a stretcher, but they didn't pump his heart or stop the bleeding, didn't do anything except for maybe mime-check his pulse. They covered him in a white sheet and filled out some paperwork. They were in no rush. When they finished with the paperwork, they rolled him over to the ambulance, started loading him in. A lady pulled up then, got out of her car, just left it running in the middle of the road, and rushed over, hysterical, maniacal, screaming: *Noooooooooooooo! My baaaaaaaaaabyyyy!* She looked about forty-five, makeup running down her face, blouse loose and blowing in the wind. She must have lived close by. Maybe she had a friend who saw the wreck on the way home from the grocery store and phoned her. *Hey, doesn't Jonathan drive a…* Or maybe it was her maternal instinct that told her something was amiss. I'll never know. But I still have dreams of the blood dripping onto his young dead face, his mother screaming into the wind and collapsing onto the asphalt. For a long time I wanted to be a paramedic. I wanted to learn all I could about emergency medicine.

I told myself the next time this happened, next time a person tried to die in front of me, I'd know what to do. I'd save them from the final kingdom and bring them back to earth. I'd be there, tapping my foot, waiting for the blood to start back through their veins—I'd bring them back the very moment the light takes them.

GHOSTS

I started seeing ghosts when I was sixteen or seventeen. Not really ghosts, it was the same ghost every time. I haven't seen him since we moved out of that house, ten years ago, but I saw him a lot while we were there. He hasn't come looking for me, and I haven't invested any time trying to locate him, either. I'm okay with that. Little kid ghosts are scary as shit. Toddler ghosts, that takes the fucking cake. I thought I was hallucinating the first time, like, not in a good way, but having a mental break or something. My heart bounced against my ribs. I couldn't breathe. What happened is I'd fallen asleep on the couch late that night. When I woke up, the TV was still on, and not three feet in front of me there was this kid looking at me, watching me sleep. I jumped up and turned on the lights. Nobody was there. I stayed awake for forty-eight hours straight, constantly looking over my shoulder and listening for the laughter of a child in all the empty rooms in the house.

AN
INFLUENTIAL
HISTORY

When the city I extol shall have perished, when the men to whom I sing shall have faded into oblivion, my words shall remain.

Said Pindar.

Said David Markson.

THE WAY WE LOVE

Sometimes you find out about things way too late. Seems unfair, but that's the way it is sometimes. For instance, a good friend of mine started dating this girl his senior year of high school. She was a real good-looking girl, too. Had red hair and really pale, freckle-free skin, just luminous— one of the nicest people around. And my friend, he was an artsy kind of guy who didn't shower regularly and had a dad with a flipper arm. Nice people all around, just two different classes coming to a head. She came from a more affluent neighborhood, so they'd spend most of the time they had together at her dad's house. Well, nothing seemed amiss to my buddy, seemed like a normal family, aside the absence of her mother, who'd died when she was little, and her dad seemed to like him okay. Her older brother had even taken a liking to him. Just like that, it happened. My buddy and his girl were getting things revved up late one night in her bedroom. I mean, the way he tells it, they were going at it hard and heavy. Right when he's about to come, the door flew open and the light flipped on. *Daddy,* she said, but her voice wasn't angry or scared or even embarrassed. *Not now, daddy, Kyle's over.* My friend, they were in missionary, had cranked around when the light flipped on. He said, *You wouldn't believe it. Her dad, he was standing there buck naked, and he was touching himself. Didn't look mad, just disappointed. At first I just chalked it up to him being drunk off his ass or something, you know. But it happened again, a few months later. But it wasn't her dad this time, it was her brother, same exact scenario. Totally fucked me up, man. After that, I talked her into moving in with me. And even still, sometimes she goes over there to spend the night. And I'm like, Are you fucking kidding me? And she's like, Well, they're my fucking family. They're all I have.*

RELEASE

My brother was released from prison today. It took some convincing from my wife, but eventually I called him. I told him, *Don't hate me, but I've been writing about you.* He said, *Hate? That's not even possible. I'm proud of you.* I said, *I love you, man. I've missed you.* He said it back. And I felt it, it pushed on me. I held in my tears the entire two hours we talked. Even when I feel like I feel all this hate in me, I realize it's just my love with nowhere to go.

I mean, no matter what happens, he'll always be my brother. He could tear my dick off and throw it out of a speeding car, let me bleed out into the center console while screaming obscenities at oncoming traffic, and I'd love him just as much as I ever have and ever will—and let me tell you, that's a whole fucking lot, and it's forever.

AN
INFLUENTIAL
FUTURE

Unless they are burned in heaps upon heaps upon heaps in a dying world, our whispers shall remain.

Said I.

Said no one.

STRANGE
FLUTTERS

It is December. You smell the chimney fires and the cold wind. The last time you heard, it was only ten degrees outside. Most winters around here are like that. You smoke a cigarette and never quite know when you are done exhaling. Your breath leaves ghostly impressions behind you, little reminders that there is a behind-the-scenes machine working overtime for your existence.

I'm six years old. It's Christmas, my mother's baking pies, and the presents have all been ripped open and strewn about the carpet in the living room. I'm wearing a Batman cape, ready to take on the day. I'm scoping my brother's new ThunderCats toys. I like mine just fine, but I always seem to like his things better. He's got Lion-O in the air, doing somersaults and backflips, kicking the shit out of a GI Joe. The TV is on, playing *A Christmas Story* or *Scrooged* or something, my dad snoozing out on the couch. I reach over for one of my brother's toys, expecting a slap, but he smiles at me, all toothy and sincere, and hands me Lion-O. *Here, we can fight the bad guys together,* he says. And I truly feel happy. I know it's only a matter of time before I'll annoy him. And then he'll take his toys back and go off to his room alone. I know things will go back to being normal—but I don't care, especially not now, not in this moment. Things are good, not bad, we are alive and living, not dead, not yet, not ever, so long as we know we'll live forever, not bad, not good, but together, sealing ourselves, here, with one last joke:

Knock, knock!

Who's there?

You.

You who?

You tell me.

Parts of this book were previously published in the following publications:

"Baptisms for the Dead" at *Hobart*

"Disney Vacation" at *Everyday Genius*

A shortened version of "A Cat Dies" called "Meat" at *Short, Fast and Deadly*

"Just Rain" at *Revolution John*

"Riots" at *NOÖ Weekly*

"Cough Syrup", "Phone Sex", and "Collapsible Lungs" at *Vol. 1 Brooklyn*

ACKNOWLEDGEMENTS

Thank you: Jamie Iredell, Michael Seidlinger, Ken Baumann, Mike Young, Scott McClanahan, J. David Osborne, and Peter Markus—for your help and guidance and friendship. Big thanks to Kevin Sampsell, publisher extraordinaire, for believing in me enough to bring this book out into the world—and for being an awesome dude and great friend.

Tina Morgan: Thanks for having the great editorial eyes you have. Your suggestions really made things pop.

Bryan Coffelt: Thanks for one of the illest book covers to ever hit a bookshelf.

Ariana Marquis: You are a wonderful publicist. Thank you, thank you, thank you, and thank you.

Chad Droegemeier: Thanks for being the best friend a guy could have. I love you, man. You took some wonderful pictures, and I'm glad they're right here in my first book.

Mom, Dad, Amanda, Paul, Cherrise, Shelli, all of my nieces and nephews: I love you more than you could ever even imagine and more.

Fran, Randy, Jane, Peter, Mat, Big Liz, and extended family: your support and love are both abundant and beautiful.

Liz: you are everything—have been since I met you and always will be, forever and always. Love you

Lightning Source UK Ltd.
Milton Keynes UK
UKHW022119180620
365222UK00019B/319